TWO STRANDS
OF LIGHT

TWO STRANDS OF LIGHT

by

Leopole A. McLaughlin, III

*****

PUBLISHED BY
Elopoel Publishing LLC

*****

TWO STRANDS OF LIGHT

Published in the United States of America

ISBN: 9781798420959
Drama/Crime/Law

* * * * *

Dedicated to K & K

Chapter 1

"All Rise!" the court clerk yells out as Judge Tate enters into the courtroom and strolls towards his seat at the bench.

We all sit back down anticipating what verdict the jury will bring to us in the next few minutes.

The courtroom was immensely quiet as we waited, and my thoughts were constantly reverberating in my head non-stop.

What the hell is taking the jury so long to get in here? Did they not tell us that they reached a verdict? Did I win? Did I lose? Is prison in the future? All sorts of shit is running through my head as I sit and wait.

After about thirty minutes the court clerk goes over to the jury room door to open it and let the jurors enter.

"All rise for the jury," she yells as she opened the door to let the jurors back into the courtroom from their deliberations. As the jurors took their seats in the jury box, everyone sat back down except for me and my client. As we stand at the Defendant table my client was shaking and stricken with fear for the outcome of the verdict. The foreman hands a folded piece of paper to the bailiff who then hands it to the judge who reads it silently to himself and then hands it back to the bailiff to give to the foreman. The judge then nods his head to the clerk who then stands up and says in a loud voice to the jury, "In the case of State of Maryland versus Angela Garcia, what is the jury's verdict?"

From the time that the clerk asked that question until the time the foreman answered seemed like an eternity had gone by.

"Not Guilty," exclaimed the foreman of the jury as he read aloud the verdict of the child neglect case of the young 23-year-old mother who has been allegedly leaving her 7-year-old son home alone for several hours while she worked at her second job.

As the verdict was read, I was so elated and excited that I could barely hold in my enthusiasm for having won the case. I felt like jumping up and pumping my fist in the air like Tiger Woods does after sinking a hole in one. As I looked over at my client, a young, frail looking, petite Hispanic woman, her tears of sorrow had turned into tears of joy.

Angela was an immigrant from Mexico whose life was full of conflict and strife. She was raped by her stepfather at age 15, gave birth at 16, then married a man at 17 who turned out to be very abusive. When she was able to gain enough strength and courage to leave him, she migrated to the states illegally. Five years after leaving Mexico she decided to settle here in Baltimore City, Maryland to raise her son.

With no other family or friends to depend upon, she felt as though she needed to do anything and everything possible that she could in order to provide for her son even if that meant leaving him home alone for a few hours while she worked at the grocery store down the street from her apartment until midnight five nights a week.

She was doing this for nearly a year until a neighbor found out that she had been leaving him home alone after he caused a small fire in the kitchen when he had fallen asleep while leaving food on the stove and the fire department had to be called by that neighbor in the adjacent apartment. She was looking at four years in prison plus deportation had she been found guilty of child neglect.

Although I work extremely hard for all my clients, this particular case was one of the most trying cases that I have had. I get emotionally vested in my clients and because of that I believe in their innocence. I pride myself on being considered one of the best and highly respected public defenders not only in Baltimore City but the entire state of Maryland. I'm like a god with the law.

Here in a city where the crime rate is a staggering 62 percent and of that 92 percent are black offenders. I am hated by many prosecutors and Baltimore City police officers however endeared by the low-income criminals that I represent. I take serious pride in my career and fully believe that the right to a lawyer is a pillar of American Jurisprudence. Unfortunately, this is a right that we have only had since 1963 when the Supreme Court ruled in Gideon versus Wainwright, where that any person who is too poor to hire a lawyer, cannot be assured a fair trial unless counsel is provided for him.

Being an African American male myself, my main purpose in life is to help as many African Americans as I can, especially Black males, obtain fair representation in a judicial system which is known to be biased, unequal and unfair. Well what better place to do so than being a public defender in a crime-stricken city like Baltimore?

"Gracias! Muchas gracias!" My client says as she embraces me, thanking me for helping her not go to prison. Her eyes were filled with joy and her soft voice now rambling not-so-quietly in Spanish. I couldn't understand her words but could only know that they were words of adulation and flattery from the sound of the praise in her voice.

I start to head out of courtroom and try to act oblivious to the stares of the many people watching me as I leave in my slightly wrinkled tailored blue pin-stripe suit, still trying to personify a debonair swagger image with a determined look on my face, however, all that is now on my mind is my next case later this afternoon and how to win it.

This is a case of a 19-year-old black male who sold a "dime" bag of marijuana to an undercover officer and was charged with a felony and is now looking at a 5-year prison sentence. Since this young man couldn't post the $5,000 bond, he must be brought to the courthouse from central booking during the afternoon "shipment" by the correctional officers at Baltimore City Central Booking.

Cases like these make me especially angry because I read somewhere that there are over one hundred and twenty thousand people who work in the cannabis industry yet last year alone, there were well over six hundred and fifty thousand people arrested for marijuana possession, mostly African-Americans.

Blacks in Baltimore City are more than five times likely to be arrested for possession for marijuana than whites even though marijuana use among both races is fairly equal. This makes Baltimore the fifth highest arrest rate for marijuana possessions in the US.

I rush out of the courthouse and into the cool brisk February air which sends a cold sensation down my back. Having forgotten my overcoat in my office, I walk very briskly in a manner to try and warm myself up as I hear my stiff leather shoes making a terrible squeaking sound as they flex against the cold, ice-laden concrete as I head back to the Public Defender's office almost two blocks away.

"Mr. Clayton! Hey, Mr. Clayton, could you hold up for a moment!"

I turn around and see a very elderly African American woman limping with a bamboo cane that is clacking onto the cracked sidewalk, trying to chase me down. I stop and turn to see what it was that she wanted.

"Can I help you ma'am?"

"Yes, yes you can." said the woman. "I saw you in court today and wanted to know if you would be able to help my grandson who is currently held at the city jail. He was arrested about two weeks ago, and has been there ever since, and no one has yet to see him regarding his charge."

"What was he charged with?" I asked.

"He was charged with gun possession and assault," explained the woman.

"Did he have a gun?"

"Well, yes, yes he did have a gun on him, but he didn't assault anyone, I just know my grandson and I know that he wouldn't of have assaulted nobody," exclaimed the woman.

"Well I'm sorry to hear this but unfortunately I don't choose my cases. They are randomly given to the Public Defenders on a revolving basis. I'm really sorry ma'am but I most likely won't get your grandson's case."

"Please sir, can't you do anything? You are the

only public defender that seems to care around here," expressed the woman.

"There's really not much that I can do, but tell you what, tell me his name and I will try to have a paralegal go to central booking to interview him so that he can be a step ahead when an attorney is assigned to him."

"Thank you, Mr. Clayton. His name is Jeremiah. Jeremiah Scott. Please see what you can do."

"I'll do my best, ma'am."

"Thank you again sir. You have a lovely blessed day."

"No problem, ma'am. You have a blessed day as well.

She then turned around and was walking unusually slowly back from where she came from, almost robotically, as if her brain was struggling to tell each foot to take the next step. It was as if her chasing me down drained every bit of energy from her little frail body.

When I finally make it to my building, I rush inside and try to avoid eye contact with anyone for fear that they may stop me and want to chat when I'm clearly in a hurry. I have one hour to pick up my new cases for the week, file the closed cases, and finish writing two briefs which were due yesterday, and then review and prepare for my afternoon case. All this while gobbling down my lunch, brushing my teeth, and of course, "handling my business" in the restroom, and then, the daily ritual of calling my wife Saundra, who seems to be just as busy at her job since she works as a corporate attorney at a large firm in Washington, DC an hour away.

With one paralegal and one secretary assigned to every three Public Defenders most basic work must be done by myself, which makes it very difficult to finish what needs to be finished on a daily basis and makes each day last more than ten hours long.

Just as I had my office key in my hand about to unlock my office door, my supervisor, Fletcher Daniels shouts out for me to come over to his office.

Fletcher is a very tall white guy, with a "buzz" haircut reminiscent of the days when he was a Marine Drill Sergeant before getting into law. He actually looks like the villain in the movie Rocky IV, Ivan Drago, but has the annoying voice of Gilbert Gottfried. I guess all that screaming in the Marines took a toll on his voice because now all I hear is the AFLAC duck when he speaks. He used to be a federal prosecutor known for his intimidating look and his many successful convictions. He is known for being very fastidious and always coerces defendants to take plea deals even if the prosecution might have a very weak case.

About seven years ago it was decided by the state that it would be better for Fletcher to lead the Public Defender's Office in order to help quickly move the influx of cases by mainly offering plea deals without the expense of having to go to trial. On average nationally, 90 – 95 percent of criminal cases end in plea bargaining. If it were only up to Fletcher, he would make sure 100 percent of cases would end with a plea deal.

"Hey Fletcher, what's going on?" I asked.

"Richard, congratulations on your case today, but we must all remember that our resources are very limited here and we should spend as little time as possible on each case in order to move on to the next case. These defendants are just looking to move quickly through the system so they can go home faster."

"Yes, I do understand what the goal is here, but shouldn't our goal also be to give our clients a good defense as well? Besides, I'm the best PD here. I didn't get that way by just bowing down to plea deals." I retorted.

"Of course, they have a right to a good defense, but let me remind you that here in the PD office we don't have the time nor the resources to do anything other than give them the best plea deal we can. We have way too many defendants coming through here every day to waste too much time on just one person," stated Fletcher.

Honestly, I have never been one to just want to give a defendant a plea deal. Back when I was in law school, I heard of a story of an African American single mother of two, by the name of Erma Faye Stewart, who was arrested in a drug sweep in Texas.

Although she maintained her innocence, her public defender told her to plead guilty, since she was facing 10 years in prison and the prosecutor only offered probation with no added jail time. Erma spent a month in jail, and then relented to a plea even though she had not committed the said crime and was consequently sentenced to 10 years' probation and was also ordered to pay a $1,000 fine.

The prosecution's case turned out to be very weak and ended up dropping all the cases of everyone who was arrested but because Erma had already plead guilty her case was not dropped like all the others and she was now considered a convicted felon. Because she now had a felony record, she was barred from getting food stamps and was evicted from her public housing home.

When she and her children became homeless, the children were taken away and placed in foster care. In the end, she had lost everything even though she took a plea for a crime that she did not commit in the hopes of saving everything.

That case had always haunted me, so after I learned of that case, I vowed never to coerce any defendant to take a plea deal, however there was just one case I had where I felt that it was in the best interest for the defendant to take a plea. It was the case of a 12-year old juvenile defendant who accidently shot his little 7-year old brother in the head with a loaded gun that the mother's boyfriend had left on a table in their house. It was clear that the boy was extremely distraught and devastated by the accidental discharge that killed his little brother and having him go to jail for the rest of his juvenile life was not at all in the best interest of anyone. The boy took the offered plea of a 10 - year probation sentence however; the mother's boyfriend was eventually charged with negligent manslaughter and was eventually given seven years in prison.

I leave Fletcher's office to finally get into my own in order to get some work done before the trial this afternoon.

In my office, there is a pile of folders on one side of my desk marked "Done" and on the other side is an even bigger pile marked, "New Cases," which never seem to go down. I glance at the pictures on my wall for a glimmer of inspiration before getting started.

On one wall is the famous 1965 picture of Muhammad Ali standing over Sonny Liston with the words underneath which states, "I am the Greatest," and on an adjacent wall is a picture of Nelson Mandela with a quote underneath Mandela's picture which states, "To deny people their human rights is to challenge their very humanity".

Then reaching into the top draw of my desk I pull out my old iPod where I blast the two songs that I use for energy and motivation; the theme song to "Rocky" which gives me motivation and then I play "Mama Said Knock You Out" by LL Cool J to give me the needed energy to knock the prosecution out.

As luck would have it, just as I was about to leave my office to head over to the courthouse for my next case, the court clerk calls to inform me that the trial had to be postponed due to an emergency that Judge Ransin, the presiding judge over the case, is having to deal with at the moment. Apparently, a defendant who he had just sentenced to 45 years in prison hit his attorney in the face then tried to jump the bench to attack the judge.

Officers grabbed the defendant just inches before he reached the judge.

I thought that this turned out to be great for me because not only was I dreading having to present in front of Judge Ransin who is known as a hard-ass prick of a judge who goes strictly by the book and is known for giving stiff sentences especially to Black offenders, but now I can settle down for a moment to get organized, call Saundra, and then leave the office early for the first time in two weeks so I can be home to hang out a little longer this evening with my 8-year old daughter, Ciana, who is the apple of my eye. It never matters how hard of a day that I may have had, when I'm with Ciana the stress and anxiety all seem to just melt away.

Chapter 2

When I get home from work my daily routine usually remains the same. Saundra thinks that I can be very predictable, although I don't really agree with her on that, however, I can sometimes see why she would think that since every day I pull up to the house and park my spotless black Mercedes in the same spot, kiss my wife and my daughter, read the mail, walk and play with the dog with Ciana; a female German Sheppard mix that I had gotten from the shelter over a year ago that we named Samantha, for about an hour, then afterwards I eat dinner, and then sit on the couch in front of the TV watching CNN as I read over my caseload until it's time for me to go to bed. The only time out of the day when my routine becomes unpredictable is when I deal with those poor criminals that I represent each day in the public defender's office which is usually a constant daily circus.

Saundra, on the other hand, is far less predictable than I am. She is the epitome of the stereotypical corporate lawyer. Extremely driven, hardnosed, ambitious, and elegant, and who usually knows what she wants and how to get what she wants from others. She lives her life day by day where spontaneity is her strong point. She has the persona of Jessica Pearson from the television show, "Suits," but has the charisma of Claire Huxtable from the "Cosby Show". Saundra's appearance is always on point, whether she is wearing a business suit or sweat clothes, she always makes sure that she is projecting an image of success. I must admit, sometimes even I sometimes feel a bit inadequate around her.

There are plenty of times when she and I bump heads and don't agree on things because she feels that one should pay for high quality legal service and believes that I am wasting my talent on Baltimore's under privileged derelicts.

"DADDY!" Ciana yells with excitement as I walk through the garage door and into the house. "I'm so happy that you're home early. How was your day?" she asks.

Ciana is such a bright beacon of light brought about through darkness. When Saundra was pregnant with Ciana, it was a very difficult pregnancy. This was her third full term pregnancy; however, the previous two ended in miscarriages during the third trimester. She and I were both very worried about this one because Ciana wasn't putting on the weight she needed. Ciana was two weeks overdue and on the day of her birth she only weighed 3 pounds and her heart had stopped beating several times. The doctor didn't think that she would survive the birth. Then just before the tiny head peaked out, it seemed as if there was a light coming out of the birth canal as Saundra was giving birth. When Ciana came out and I had to cut the umbilical cord, it seemed as if she was encompassed in a warm bright light. So, it was that day that I found a name that was warm and meant light, 'Ciana!'

I could be having one of the worst days ever but as soon as I see and talk to Ciana it's like all the darkness and despair just seems disappears. She brings so much joy and happiness into my life. I've always believed that God had strategically placed her into my life and gave me exactly what I wanted in a child. Our bond is so strong that I never knew that I could feel a love this strong and deep before.

"I'm doing great now that I see you! How's my beautiful girl doing? How was school today?" I ask her as I'm picking her up to hug her.

"It was okay." she states. "Dad, I have to think of a science project to do and tell my teacher by next Monday. Can you help me with this?"

"Of course I will, Baby Girl! We'll work on it together this weekend."

"Thanks, Dad!"

"Let's get ready to walk Samantha."

"Ok Daddy!"

Believe it or not, walking Samantha with Ciana is always one of my best highlights of my day. This is a time when she and I strengthen our bond. She tells me her dreams, desires, and any issues that she may have, and I tell her my dreams and desires. We walk and talk and play catch with Samantha. It is remarkable how some of the simplest, modest elements of life so often taken for granted could become the catalyst for an entirely new life.

After finishing dinner as I start to read over my cases for the next day, Saundra comes to me enthusiastically and starts to discuss a litigation position that had opened up at her firm.

"Honey, I was given word today from John that we are going to strengthen our litigation department, and he suggested that you would be a great candidate for our firm. I think that it would be great if we both worked for Scranton because if we both were to eventually make partner, we would have a majority share of the firm. This could take us to a whole new level in life. Don't you think?" she asks.

"Thanks Saundra, but you know that this doesn't really interest me. Hadn't we discussed this before?" I reply clearly annoyed.

"Richard, you have been working for the PD office for the past 10 years and you are overworked, underappreciated and definitely, underpaid." Saundra exclaims.

"You're definitely right about that, I can't argue with that statement, but this is my purpose. There has to be someone who cares about the under privileged and I truly believe that God made this my purpose," I explain to her.

"So, your life's purpose is to work for the Baltimore City's Public Defenders office??" she asks clearly bewildered.

"No, of course not. My purpose is to help others who don't have the means or a voice through the justice system, somewhat as Thurgood Marshall had done. Look, just tell him that I'm not interested at the moment, besides you know when I leave PD I'm thinking about possibly getting into the political arena."

"I understand that," Saundra replies. "However, I am just looking out for our future. My parents struggled when they put me and my sister through school and they struggled when they retired, I just don't want that to happen to us. Ciana shouldn't have to worry about anything when she goes to college."

"Babe, I promise you that we will never have to struggle. Just believe me and I will not let you down," I confide to her.

"You know that I trust you and believe in you. I

just don't want us to miss out on any opportunities, but I understand and will let John know tomorrow."

"Thanks Babe."

I met Saundra about 15 years ago when we both were first year law students at Georgetown University Law School in Washington, DC. I can remember when I first saw her in my Legal Writing class. When she walked into the room, my whole world slowed down, and I felt my heart beating intensely through my chest. She was the most beautiful girl I'd ever seen yet she had a kind of understated beauty, perhaps it was because she was so disarmingly unaware of her intimidating look. Her black skin was completely flawless, with the type of face that didn't need makeup. Her curly brown hair laid effortlessly on her bare shoulders, lightly touching the straps of her one-piece dress which caressed her incredibly beautiful fit body. She exuded such an inner beauty as well that one could feel her presence in the room without even looking at her. When she smiled and laughed you couldn't help but smile along too, even if it was just on the inside. To be in her company was to feel that you too were someone, that you had been warmed in summer rays regardless of the season. This was the girl, the girl that I knew would change the way I looked at life.

Being a native Washingtonian, I always knew that Georgetown was the school for me. It is funny because even though she is from St. Louis, Missouri she also always knew that Georgetown was the school for her as well. There was always a mutual attraction between us when we first met during our first day of law school, but we had never enacted upon our attraction for one another until our third year while working on a mock trial case together. I had always found her to be very smart and beautiful and I later found out that she always found me to be very warm, charming, caring, and handsome. We seemed to be the perfect match. Both attractive, smart, and wannabe attorneys.

Back then, we were both very spontaneous and passionate about the law. We both wanted to use the law to help put an end to injustice. As far as I can remember I always loved being able to help people who were less fortunate. I always believed that the poor didn't have a fair chance in the legal system, so that is why I became a public defender in order to be able to give back. The pay is horrible but at least the feeling of accomplishment was always well worth the sacrifice of less money. Ironically, Saundra no longer felt that same way once we graduated. She became a highly motivated corporate attorney, who is now striving for partnership at her firm, Scranton Beckford & McCoy. She believes that one must pay a high price for high quality legal services. After graduation and passing the bar exam, Saundra decided that money and advancement was far more important to her than any type of advocacy.

She and I had gotten married right after we found out that we had passed the bar exam the second time around. We figured that this would be a good celebratory gift for us passing the bar, since we both were very devastated for failing the first time that we took it. Of course, no one was surprised about our marriage since we were both very much alike. Everyone who knew the both of us believed that God made us for each other. During our wedding I sung "You for Me," by Johnny Gill while she walked up the aisle towards me because it was the only song that 100% described our feelings for one another.

We both have helped each other stay on the course that we set out for, no matter how rough the journey was. Although we don't 100% agree with one another sometimes, we both always support the decisions that we each make. God has definitely blessed me with her, and I would not be who I am without her. We are definitely each other's soulmate and best friend.

"Hey honey," I start to say to her as she is cleaning up in the kitchen, "I'm sorry about our disagreement about the job and I do understand why you don't like where I work, but always remember that I do love you very much and everything I do is for you and Ciana."

She gives me a small smile but continues to wash the dishes. I then pull out my iPod and play Christina Perri's song, "A Thousand Years," then take her hand, hold her, and dance. As we dance in the kitchen, I secretly hoped that time would stand still. I couldn't ask for a more perfect way to end our evening.

Chapter 3

As I woke up to get out of bed, I had this unusual feeling of being exuberant about my upcoming day. Usually when I wake up in the morning my mind would try to grip onto the final moments of my dreams or I would lethargically get up constantly thinking about my case load and which unfortunate criminals I would have to represent that day, but today just seemed to be very different. I felt a sense of euphoric energy which felt like a high in which nothing could bring me down.

Not really knowing what was causing this euphoric feeling, I begin to think about my caseload. Today, a DUI, an assault, a mugging, and a prostitution case. Nothing exciting there. At least I can look forward to the judge who would be hearing my cases today. Judge Winslow, a very nice funny man who realizes that people do make mistakes and bad decisions in life and believes that people always need a second chance, sometimes even a third or fourth. However, although Judge Winslow is nice, he is also very fair. He has no problem doing what's right even if that means sending someone to jail.

When I got into my office it was about 8:00am on the dot and as soon as I sat down at my desk, my secretary Monica comes rushing into my office.

"Richard, Cathy is out sick today, so I was told to ask you if you would be able to take her cases in court today," exclaimed Monica.

"I already have four cases today, how many cases does she have?"

"She only has two and they are both in the afternoon."

"What are they?" I ask.

"Well the first case is a domestic violence protective order hearing and the second is a bail review hearing. Both cases are before Judge White," she explains.

Judge White is a very tough judge who hates domestic violence cases because she was once abused by her ex-husband before she got into the law. It was always thought that she had gotten into law in order to retaliate against men because of what her ex-husband had done to her. It's almost as if she has some kind of a personal vendetta against all men.

"Is there anyone else that can take her caseload today?" I ask her.

"I'm sorry Richard but you and Cathy are the only two PDs that were going to be in District Court today. The other PDs are in Circuit Court," she says.

"Ok, damn, I'll take them Monica. Please let the Court know so that I can be listed as an attorney on record"

"Thanks Richard, I'll do that, and I will also let the clerk know that you will be filling in for Cathy."

Court today seemed to be overly crowded. It was so crowded today that not only were there no more seats in the courtroom and people had to stand against the wall, but people were also lined up outside the courtroom door. Was there a full moon out this past weekend where everyone decided to commit a crime or something? And out of all the days, I had to take on another PD's caseload when it's crowded. Well at least it's not too bad since I am starting the day out in

Judge Winslow's courtroom. This might brighten up the day in order to prepare for this afternoon's terror.

Two hours went by before my first case was called. "Case number 19004821 in reference to the State of Maryland versus Charles Daniels," yelled the clerk. A white clean-cut man in his 50's wearing a very expense suit stood alongside me at the defense table. If it wasn't known better, one might have thought that the white guy was the attorney and I was the defendant.

"Your Honor," exclaims the prosecutor, "When Mr. Daniels was stopped by law enforcement driving his vehicle on North Charles Street for swerving between lanes, the officer found that he had a blood alcohol level of .04. This is his second DUI in the past two years. The statue states that on the second offence it is a mandatory 30-day incarceration period. State believes that this judgment should be imposed."

"Your Honor," I interject, "My client should not be imposed the 30-day incarceration period in which the State is recommending because his prior was actually over two years ago and was not the cause of alcohol consumption and since that time he has not gotten into any trouble with the law. My client is a law-abiding citizen with a family and has a very good job. He has already served 3 days in jail and any additional time would not benefit him but would only do more damage than it is worth. I ask for time served and probation.

"I'll accept the defense's position. Time served and 6 months' probation," stated Judge Winslow.

Great! One down, five to go!

As I finished up my caseload, I thank God that all of my cases went pretty quickly and smoothly but I still ended up rushing to get to Judge White's courtroom in order to handle Cathy's cases.

When I got into the courtroom there were only two people sitting in the pews in the courtroom. A man and a woman each on opposite sides of the room were waiting for their domestic violence protective order hearing to take place.

"Good afternoon, Your Honor. I'm Richard Clayton in for Attorney Cathy Ingram for the bail hearing and the protective order cases. I'm sorry I'm late. I had several other cases today.

"Good afternoon, Mr. Clayton." replies Judge White. "Let's get started. Let's start with the bail hearing first."

The bailiff opens the prisoner entrance to have the correctional officer bring the defendant into the courtroom.

A very large African man who stood nearly 6'5" weighing over 300lbs with multiple tattoos on his face and arms comes strolling confidently into the courtroom handcuffed and shackled accompanied by three correctional officers.

He stared at me with such an intense, menacing look, I first wondered if he thought that I was the prosecutor and not the public defender who is here to help him. If he was trying to be intimidating it definitely worked.

He sat down next to me still handcuffed as the judge read off his charges.

"Good afternoon, Mr. Darion Tibbs. This is a bail review hearing in which I will read off your charges and decide whether to grant bail or whether to keep the commissioner's recommendation of No Bail. Do you understand, Mr. Tibbs?" asked the judge.

Darion doesn't respond but just looks at the judge with the same intensity that he looked at me.

"I need a 'yes' or a 'no' Mr. Tibbs."

Still no answer with a continued stare.

"Your Honor," I interject, "May I have a moment to confer with my client?"

"Yes you may, Mr. Clayton."

"Mr. Tibbs," I whisper to him so that no one can hear our conversation. "Do you understand what the judge is saying and that this is a bail review hearing?"

"I hear her, I just don't give a fuck." He retorts in a deep baritone voice.

"Would you like me to respond on your behalf and then explain anything that you might not understand to you?" I ask.

"Did you hear what I just said? I don't give a fuck."

"Your Honor, my client does understand that this is a bail review hearing. I will be responding on his behalf and if there is anything that he doesn't understand I shall explain it to him." I say to Judge White.

"That will be fine. Mr. Tibbs, you have four charges against you. I base my decision on bail by four different factors. First, I look at the seriousness of the charge, second, I will look at your previous criminal history if there is any. Third, I will consider if you are a flight risk, and forth, I will look at whether you pose a danger or a threat to public safety. Do you understand, Mr. Tibbs?"

I turn to my client for a second then turned back. "Yes, my client does understand." I say to the judge.

"Mr. Tibbs, your charges are as follows: Count number one, attempted murder in the first degree, which carries a maximum penalty of life. Count number two, aggravated assault, which carries up to 25 years. Count number three, kidnapping, which carries up to 30 years. Count number four, unlawful possession of a firearm, which carries 3 years. Do you understand the charges set before you, Mr. Tibbs?"

I turn to my client for a second then turn back to the judge. "Yes, my client does understand the charges." I tell her.

"I am setting bail at $250,000. Mr. Clayton, I know that you are just filling in for Ms. Ingram, however, I am going to remove her as counsel and appoint you as his counsel. Ok?"

"Yes, Your Honor."

"We betta not lose, you bitch azz nigga. I know muthafuckas. Memba that." Darion whispers to me before he stands up to go back with the officers.

Did this mother fucker just threaten me? What the fuck?? I'm trying to help him and he goes and threatens me!

"Nah Brah, it don't work like that." Speaking to him loud enough where mostly everyone could hear. "I don't have to do shit for you. As a matter of fact, go and find an attorney who will be intimidated by you. I'm not the one. Fuck you."

Judge White just looks at the whole ordeal but doesn't say a word. This is probably why the judge removed Cathy. Cathy probably wasn't really sick, she was scared. Alright, whatever.

The two individuals who were waiting for their domestic violence protective order is still waiting in the courtroom.

When the clerk called their case, the man who was having the order placed on him just came to the table and told the judge that he decided not to fight the order but just to consent to it. Then Judge White just signed the order and sent him on his way.

Thank God my day in court is finally over. After finishing up some work in my office I'll be able to leave the office by about 7:30pm today. Well at least it's not 8:00pm. I always try never to do a straight twelve hours in one day. That's where I draw the line.

Leaving the office this evening it is a bit dark outside, so I always try to walk fast and am always aware of my surroundings.

In my car I keep a handgun in the glove compartment which is always fully loaded with two .45 long colt bullets and three 410 gauge shot shells. It's the Taurus Judge Poly - a 5 shot revolver made by Taurus named the Judge because judges have been known to carry this type of gun under their robes in court. I had started carrying this gun with me in my car ever since I was punched in the face and knocked out by a disgruntled client's boyfriend because the man's girlfriend had to spend 6 years in prison. Even though she was looking at over 45 years in prison for attempted murder for throwing boiling oil on her boyfriend's ex-girlfriend's face as she slept, I was able to get her charge down to aggregated assault and a 6-year sentence with time served, but he was still not happy with that. He wanted her to get totally off.

I make it to my car in a timely manner and sit in it for a little while as the engine heats up and my seat warms up my backside. Sitting there I become a bit disappointed realizing that by the time I will get home it will be too late to have Ciana walk with me when I walk Samantha. Well I guess there will be plenty of times that we will be able to walk together, so why get disappointed, besides today's Friday.

Chapter 4

"Ciana?" I say as I am shaking her as she lays in her bed. "It's Saturday morning, wanna go walk and play with me and Samantha outside? It looks like a nice brisk sunny day today, so if you get dressed and put on your coat you can come join us."

"Okay Dad."

"Can you be ready in 20 minutes?" I ask.

"Yes, I can be up and dressed by then," replies Ciana.

"Cool. Come downstairs when you're ready."

"Okay."

Ciana comes running down the stairs after thirty minutes with her curly, frizzy brown hair pulled back in a bun and wiping off some toothpaste stuck in the corner of her month.

It was a nice brisk sunny morning as the moderate breeze hits us from behind as we walked Samantha to the dog park.

"So, what were your two highs and one low at school yesterday?" I ask her as I always do every day. I always start the conversation by asking Ciana that question every day in order to find out what her two high points of the day were and a one low point that she may have had.

"Um, well, one of my high points was that I got an A on my spelling test yesterday." stated Ciana.

"Wow, that's great! Good job! Good for you! What's the other high?" I cheered.

"The other high is that we had an open day in gym."

"An open day? What does that mean?" I ask.

"It is a day where we can do whatever sport we like to do. So, they set up the gym area with different things to do, like one corner was for doing gymnastics on the mats, and another area was for playing basketball, there was also an area for volleyball and soccer." replied Ciana.

"That sounds fun! Which one did you do?"

"I played one game of volleyball and two games of basketball."

"Okay, cool. So now, what was your low?" I ask.

"Well I guess my low would be that my homeroom teacher was absent, so we had to have a substitute teacher."

"What, you didn't like her or something? Was she mean to the kids?"

"No, she wasn't mean, she was okay. I just like Mrs. Sanders better. So, what were your two highs and a low yesterday?" she asked.

"Well, my low was not being home early enough to hang out with you. And, let's see, my first high was that my cases went well and moved quickly through the process and the second high was finishing my day in less than twelve hours." I stated to her emphatically.

"Dad, I have another question for you."

"Shoot."

"What were your desires and goals that you wanted to do when you were a kid, and do you have any new dreams that you want now?"

I am always amazed at some of the questions Ciana asks me and am sometimes surprised at how mature and intelligent that she is.

"Wow, that's some question there. What made you come up with a question like that?"

"Well it was a question that the substitute teacher had asked all of us yesterday."

"Well, when I was a kid, I wanted to be a policeman. My father had told me that being a policeman was not a good job and to think of something else. Then a few years later I wanted to be a doctor and then my father told me that I wasn't smart enough to become a doctor because I didn't get good grades. Never let anyone tell you that you can't do something, not even me. If you believe in yourself, that's all that matters. Understand?"

"Yes, I understand."

"Aside from that, now let's see, besides my idea of running for Governor of Maryland," I jokingly laugh, "I had a new idea of being able to start a non-profit organization with top notch attorneys to help give under-privileged individuals top tier representation without thinking about having to always take a plea deal."

"That seems interesting," she states. "What made you come up with that idea?"

"Well, several years ago, I read this statement by Angela Davis which inspired me," I tell her. "Do you know who she is?"

"No, who is she?" she replies.

"Well she was a civil rights activist back in the '60s and '70s. She's still alive today but just not as active as she once was. Well anyway, she noted that, if the number of people exercising their trial rights suddenly doubled or tripled in some jurisdictions, it would create chaos in the judicial system. I believe that. If defendants weren't afraid to always fight, the prosecutors would be fairer regarding their decisions in judgments."

"I think that's a great idea, Dad," she says.

"You think all my ideas are great. Even the bad ones," I laugh.

"Well I believe in you, Dad,"

"Thanks Sweetheart. I believe in you too! So, what are your new dreams and desires," I then ask her.

"I want to start a doggie day care when summer gets here," she replies.

"Oh really! That's cool! Why a doggie day care?"

"Well I think that Samantha gets lonely being home alone all day when I'm at school and when you and mom are at work, and there must be a lot of other dogs that may feel lonely too. So why not have them all together doing something?"

"Hmm, you make a good point there. I like that. Very good idea. Now you just have to figure out how to implement your idea in order to manifest your dream." I say.

"Yes, I know. Can you help me with this?" she asks.

"Of course! Maybe if we have time later today, we can write up the idea, but we have to work on your school science project first. That cool?"

"Yeah, that's cool."

"Do you have any ideas for the science project yet?" I ask.

"No, not really. Can you think of anything?"

"Hmm, let's see. How about an erupting volcano?" I say excitingly.

"That would be cool! How do we make it?"

"We would use molding clay for the mountain, and then get some paint to make it look rocky."

"How would we be able to make it erupt?"

"Baking soda and vinegar will do the trick and if that doesn't work, we'll just pop a couple of Mentos in some Coke. Works every time."

"Cooool! I can't wait to do it." Ciana says elatedly.

"I can't wait either."

The walk, talk and play, went on for over an hour, and by the time we came back in the house with Samantha, Saundra has breakfast cooking in the kitchen.

"Great, y'all are back! Had a good walk?" Saundra asks.

"Yes mom, it was good," Ciana states.

"What do y'all talk about?" Saundra asks as she smiles and looks at me.

"Life," I say laughing. "Just life."

Chapter 5

When I got into my office Monday morning, I found myself to be a little exhausted by all the fun and the excitement that I had with Saundra and Ciana during the weekend. When I go to grab a cup of espresso from the Krups machine in the office kitchen, Monica comes up to me carrying several folders in her hands. The never ending, constantly growing pile of cases.

"Hey Richard! How was your weekend," Monica asks?

"Actually, it went very well. I just chilled with my family," I stated. "How was yours?"

"It was okay, nothing spectacular," she replies.

"You seem like you could be a fun person, I'm sure every weekend is spectacular for you," I tell her smiling.

"You always seem to know the right things to say," she laughs. "Well today I'll give you a choice of your caseload. I have here a mugging, a murder, and an assault"

When I look at the files in her hand, I notice that the assault case folder looks the thinnest.

"What's the name on the assault case?"

"Hmm, let's see…Scott. Jeremiah Scott." Monica states.

"Oh wow! His grandmother came up to me a couple of weeks ago asking me if I could help him out. I think I'll go ahead and take that one."

"Here you go," she states as she passes the folder to me. "The preliminary hearing is tomorrow morning at 9:30 in courtroom 203."

"Thanks Monica. I'll go visit him this afternoon at central booking."

I went back into my office and began to read the Scott file that was handed to me.

[On January 26, at 3:00pm, a Black male, later identified as Jeremiah Scott, was walking around the Royal Farms convenient store at the corner of North Avenue and Pennsylvania Avenue acting very suspiciously. As he decided to leave the store for apparently noticing that he was being watched, he got into an altercation with an Indian man (name withheld) as he was walking out, who stated that Scott bumped into him harshly and then pulled a gun on him because he (Indian man) was in his (Scott) way. The Indian man then walked away as he was dialing 911 for police assistance. Baltimore City Police Officer Browning spotted and identified Scott walking two blocks away going west on North Avenue away from the scene. Officer Browning noticed Scott acting very edgy and agitated, so he asked Scott to place his hands on the hood of his squad car. Scott was reluctant to comply, so the officer withdrew his service weapon and pointed it at Scott. Scott then complied with the officer's command and through a thorough body search, an unloaded 9mm Beretta was found in Scott's belt buckle. He was then arrested on the spot and sent to Baltimore City Central Booking.]

When I read the brief, I noticed that there were a few inconsistencies in the report which didn't seem to add up. It was inundated with extraneous facts with the intention of obfuscating the case. However, I decided not to infer until I heard from Scott himself.

I stared at the mug shot of Jeremiah and the picture of the gun that the officer had confiscated located in the file. Actually, Jeremiah didn't look like the typical street thug. He looked as though he was pulled right off of a college campus. He would totally fit in at the University of Maryland or at Morgan State. Very clean cut with his hair parted on the left side, wearing a light blue buttoned-up collared shirt. Although this defendant didn't fit the typical mold of a street thug, I did know that I have been in this business long enough not to judge a book by its cover. I've once had a case where a grandmother who looked like she should be baking cookies was actually known for baking bricks of crack cocaine.

There is usually only one day out of the week where I don't have to be in court for trial and today just so happened to be that day. I'm very glad about this because now I can catch up on the overdue briefs of my previous cases and spend the day meeting defendants at the jail, which is something usually only privately paid criminal defense attorneys seem to do. I think Jeremiah is due a visit from me.

When I get to the jail, I find a parking space on the left side of BCCB next to the Jones Falls Expressway which runs from downtown into the county. BCCB is a large pale, insipid tan building with the words above the door stating; Baltimore City Central Booking and Intake Center. It is the first building offenders are brought to when they commit a crime in Baltimore City. Offenders were only supposed to stay here no more than two weeks before being sent to the city jail located next door in an old dark gray, decrepit facility which looks like the Castle Grayskull building in the old He-Man cartoons, but a couple of years ago the Governor decided to close down that facility due to it being antiquated and its porous security invited rampant smuggling of contraband, and in its final years Baltimore's notorious gang, the Black Guerrilla Family, virtually ran the institution. Closing this facility down left no other options to house offenders, so now BCCB is seriously, dangerously overcrowded and houses everyone from simple petty theft to murder.

As I walked through the large metal doors of the facility, I could smell the stench of cheap perfume and pine sol which clouded the air. Two metal detectors are by the door, but only one of them is manned by a frumpy looking correctional officer who resembles Barney Rubble from the Flintstones. There is a second correctional officer who is looking onward as visitors place their items on the conveyor belt of the x-ray machine.

"Hello. Please remove your jacket, belt and your watch and put them in the tray," the frumpy officer states.

"No problem," I retort.

"Are you an attorney seeing a client or are you just here to visit a friend or a family member," asked the second correctional officer in a very deep baritone voice.

"I am legal counsel for an inmate named Jeremiah Scott," I tell him.

"Ok, just sign here with your bar card number and he will meet you in the legal room located in Dorm number 7," stated the second correctional office. "Do you know how to get there?"

"Yes, I'm familiar where it is. I'll wait there for him, thank you," I replied.

When I finally make it through all the secured doors through the maze-like halls to Dorm number 7, a guard lets me into the dormitory which houses about 70 inmates all in one big area with an overflow of bunk beds. The stench of strong bad body odor mixed with the smell of the overuse of Lysol overwhelms the area. The legal room is at the front left of the dorm past the guard's desk which is manned by only two correctional officers. I wait in the room as the guard calls for Jeremiah to go to the legal room for a legal visit. As I sit and wait for Jeremiah to come into the room, I look around at the faces of the men in the dormitory. Some faces show fear, others show anger, and there are even some faces that don't show anything at all. Almost as if they're in the comfort of their own living room at home.

A tall, lanky young African American man in a yellow jumpsuit comes strolling in the room.

"Hello, how are you? I'm Mr. Clayton, the attorney who will be representing you," I state as I stand up and stretch out my hand for a handshake.

"I'm good," says Jeremiah.

"Can you tell me what happened," I ask
Jeremiah sits down slumped over, clearly agitated and frustrated.

"I don't think it really fucken matters what I say, they gonna say that I did that shit anyways," says Jeremiah.

"Well I'm asking you, what is your version of what happened," I say to him.

"Simple. I was in Royal Farms…and was reaching up to get a magazine which was on the top shelf. When I reached up, my gun showed in my waste. Some Indian looking dude saw my gun so when I notice him looking at me, I jetted out. Then I noticed that he was following me when I was outside, so I turned around and shouted for him to stop fucken following me. That's it. Two blocks down the street a goddamn cop pulls up on me in his car as I was walking and tells me to put my hands on the hood of his car. He handcuffs me and takes my gun and arrests me," stated Jeremiah.

"Did you ever pull the gun?"

"No, never," stated Jeremiah.

"Where did you get the gun from? Is it registered?"

"It used to be Pop pop's gun. It's registered to him."

"Who is Pop pop?

"My grandfather."

"Did you resist the officer's arrest?" I asked.

"Yo, you fucken kidding me? Of course not. I did everything what that fucken cop said. I ain't trying to be the next fucken Freddie Gray," Jeremiah said referring to the African-American man who was accidentally killed by Baltimore city police while being transported for an arrest for possessing a legal pocketknife. His death started a peaceful protest in April 2015, and then the protest turned very violent which resulted in the worst rioting, looting, and the desecration of the city seen since the riots in '68.

"What's the highest level of education that you have?" I ask him.

"I dropped out in the 11th grade."

"Why did you drop out?"

"Cause I ain't seen nothing for me there. My moms was a drug fiend and my pops left when I was 3 and I ain't seen that nigga since, so why would I go there."

"So you were raised by your grandmother?"

"Yeah, she and my grandfather raised me."

"She actually chased me down a few weeks ago trying to get me to take your case. Evidentially, she really believes in you."

"Ha, that's Nanny." Jeremiah chuckles.

"Look Jeremiah, I'm going to speak frank with you for a moment. You are 19 years old and are still very young and have your whole life ahead of you. Regardless of whatever happens here on this case, you still have a decision as to what path you can go in your life. Realize though that each path has very different outcomes. You can either continue on the path that you're on and end up stuck in this revolving door, or you can start realizing your self-worth and do better for yourself. The choice is yours. Understand?" I stated firmly.

"Yeah, I guess so." He says as he shrugs his shoulders.

"No son! Do you understand?" I state in a more strong and forceful voice staring dead in his eyes.

"Yes, yes sir. I do understand." He says more alert this time staring right back in my eyes with a sense of caring.

"Ok, Mr. Scott. I will talk to the prosecutor tomorrow before our prelim and see what they have. I will try to get it dropped based on lack of evidence, but of course, there is no guarantee for that," I say.

"Alright, thank you," stated Jeremiah as he gets up from his seat to return to the main area of the dorm.

As I get up and gathered my things, I hear a very loud noise coming from the dormitory which startles me so much that I end up dropping my paperwork onto the floor.

A fight broke out in the dorm where these three black men are beating up on this one Hispanic man. The Hispanic man was fighting back at first but after realizing that being outnumbered, he was definitely at a severe disadvantage, he goes into a ball fetal position on the floor while the other men continue beating and stomping on him.

An officer then tells me to stay put inside the legal room while they call for other officers on their radios to come to the unit and intervene, however, I step out and continue to watch the fight. The fighting inmates seem oblivious of the officers in the dorm and seem not to even care knowing that more officers will be coming in shortly.

As the fight intensifies one of the inmates pulls out a silver item from his pocket and start stabbing the inmate who is balled up on the floor. I just stand and watch in amazement never having witnessed someone being, "shanked" before except on tv or the movies where you know that it's not real. Now I am actually witnessing this firsthand and realizing just how dangerous this jail really is.

About seven or eight more correctional officers wearing tactical riot armor come rushing through the dormitory's door and pins the three aggressors to the floor while the inmate who was being attacked lies restless in a pool of blood, hopelessly helpless.

I stand stunned in a moment of temporary shock. When I unfreeze my stare and get back a grip on reality and where I am, I notice that everyone just goes back to normal as if nothing ever happened. Inmates and guards just walking past the injured man who is still laying on the floor in a pool of blood, as if he were invisible until the medics come in with a stretcher to remove him.

It is obvious that inmate on inmate violence and any nefarious acts in here are just the norm and an everyday thing. I then gather all of my paperwork and then walk out of the dorm back through the maze of halls to leave the facility to head back to the "calmness" of the PD office.

Chapter 6

I arrived at the criminal circuit court on Calvert Street at 8:50 am. Luckily the circuit court is only a short walk from my office, so I feel safe getting there about 10 minutes before court starts, unlike the district court which is uptown where I would have to drive early enough to find parking.

When I got through the metal detector, I noticed from the electronic docket monitor on the wall that the prelim will be in courtroom 205 and not courtroom 203 which is stated on one of the documents. Before going into the courtroom, I sit on the bench in the lobby right outside the doors of the courtroom. As I'm sitting there, I'm looking over my notes contemplating how to proceed with the case. My goal is to prove that the state lacks the necessary evidence to proceed with a trial and to have the case dismissed, realizing though that this usually never really happens. The state would rather proceed with a weak case in the hopes that the defendant would take a plea agreement instead of dropping a case all together. These racks up prosecutors' conviction rate which makes them look good, as if they are doing their part in fighting crime.

As I take a moment to gather my thoughts before going into the courtroom to check in with the clerk, I actually notice something that I haven't really ever paid attention to before. As I'm sitting here, I look around the corridor noticing that despite the fact that this courthouse was renamed back in the 80s after the civil rights activist, Clarence M. Mitchell Jr., every imagery in the building exemplified white supremacy.

The big mural on the wall in the lobby depicted a

group of Indians on the one side and a group of Pilgrims on the other side and they come together in the middle as if they were negotiating a deal. However, the Indians in the picture are very scantily dressed in loincloth over their genitalia and a piece of cloth over their chests whereas the pilgrims where heavily fully dressed wearing a lot of fancy garments. The way the Indians are dressed, one might think that it is summertime, however, the way the Pilgrims are dressed, one might think that it is wintertime. The mural makes no sense unless it is supposed to show the superiority of one race over another.

Also, there are many sketches of previous trials on various corridor walls throughout the building where black defendants are in front of white judges and white lawyers. And in every courtroom, there are portraits on the walls of white judges who reigned in the building back in the early 1900s. I started to wonder if anyone else had notice this. I notice that I was starting to get fixated on this issue and was getting somewhat upset. After 10 years of coming into this building I couldn't understand why I am now just 'seeing' this imagery. I felt like Neo in the movie The Matrix when Neo is finally able to read and understand the hidden code in the illusion that everyone is oblivious to in the real world. I really think that this needs to change. The austere look of this courthouse is intentionally designed to subliminally intimidate the many black offenders that come in and out of its doors.

This newfound realization had intensified my fierceness as I walked into the courtroom like a knight walking into the dragon's lair determined to slay the dragon.

I sit at the defense table waiting for my client to be brought in by the jail's correctional officers and the bailiff. A clankity chain noise is coming from behind the door that is behind the left side of the judge's bench, then the noise stops and in walks Jeremiah with two officers, wearing the bright yellow BCCB jail jumpsuit that I saw him wearing yesterday at the jail. Jeremiah then walks to the defense table and sits in a chair next to me.

"All Rise," shouts the clerk. Everyone stands up as Judge MacArthur walks into the courtroom through the other door on the right side of the judge's bench and then sits down on his "throne."

"Is Mr. Scott prepared to enter a plea to the charges at this time?" asked Judge MacArthur.

"Yes," I say. "He is pleading not guilty."

"Mr. Scott, I am going to read the charges off to you and need you to tell me how you plea. On count number one, the charge of aggregated assault, which carries a sentence of up to 25 years imprisonment, how do you plea?" asked the judge.

"Not guilty," stated Jeremiah.

"On count number two, the charge of first-degree assault, which carries a sentence of up to 25 years imprisonment, how do you plea?" asked the judge.

"Not guilty," stated Jeremiah.

"On count number three, the charge of carrying an unregistered firearm, which carries a sentence of up to 10 years imprisonment, how do you plea?" the judge asked.

"Not guilty," stated Jeremiah.

"On count number four, the charge of carrying a concealed weapon, which carries a sentence of up to

10 years imprisonment how do you plea?" asked the judge.

"Not guilty," stated Jeremiah.

"And on count number five, the charge of resisting arrest, which carries a sentence of up to 3 years imprisonment, how do you plea?" asked the judge.

"Not guilty," stated Jeremiah.

"Your Honor," Ms. Clark, who is the prosecutor in this case, starts, "these are very serious charges which makes this a very serious case. However, the state is willing to offer a plea agreement of 18 months incarceration and a 2-year probation with time served."

"Would the defense like to take this offer?" asked the Judge. "If counsel needs a few minutes to consult this over with his client I can give you a few minutes."

"No thank you, Your Honor, defense doesn't need time to discuss. Defense will not be taking this offer." I state. "Actually, what we would like to do is to have this case dropped all together."

"On what grounds do you wish to have the charges dropped?" asked the judge.

"Well first", I begun forcefully, still holding onto the anger of my new-found revelation. "There is no culpable mens rea here. Mr. Scott wasn't shoplifting, he didn't rob the witness, nor was he running away from some crime scene. This is all indirectly stated in the report. As you know, the mens rea requirement is premised upon the idea that one must possess a guilty state of mind and be aware of his or her misconduct. My client was just trying to buy something in the store. You can't stop someone on suspicion! Second, if we go through these trumpery charges, I will prove to you right now that it is virtually impossible for us to even have a case here. I believe that the state recognizes that their case is very weak which is why they are offering such a plea deal.

With Count One, aggregated assault. Aggregated assault is not an actual Maryland statue. It is a term used by Maryland State Police as an unlawful attack by one person upon another for the purpose of inflicting severe or aggravated bodily injury. This charge would have been dropped regardless if we were going forward and replaced with First Degree Assault, which is already Count Number Two. And to have first degree assault, there must be some bodily harm done. Here, there was no bodily harm done so Counts One and Two must automatically be dropped. Count Number Three, carrying an unregistered firearm. First off, the firearm was not unregistered. Although it was not registered to my client it was, however, registered to his grandfather. Hypothetically, even if it were an unregistered firearm why is my client charged with a different statue that should not apply to him. The maximum penalty for an unregistered firearm charge is 10 years imprisonment IF and only IF the firearm is a prohibited firearm or pistol. It is only five years imprisonment in any other case. The firearm retrieved is not prohibited by the state of Maryland. Also, a first offender in Maryland convicted of carrying a handgun is guilty of a misdemeanor and faces a maximum potential jail term of only three years. My client is charged with a statue that states for 10 years imprisonment even though this would have been his first offense. With Count Number Four, carrying a concealed weapon. Again, my client was charged with a statue that does not imply to him. This would have been his first offense. Penalties for first offenders include up to 3 years in jail and fines ranging from $250 to $2,500, not the 10 years which is implied. And as far as Count Number Five is concerned; resisting arrest. The arrest itself must be lawful in the first place. This was not a lawful arrest. There was absolutely no real probable cause here. So, I ask that in reference to all these facts, Your Honor, I ask that this case to be dropped."

"Counsel, do you have anything to say regarding what Mr. Clayton presented?" asked the judge referring to Ms. Clark.

"Ahh, No, Your Honor. I was not aware of these facts. This case was just recently handed to me by another prosecutor" stated Ms. Clark.

"Well, I will go ahead and drop this case without prejudice." stated Judge MacArthur.

"Thank you, Your Honor," I stated elastically.

Jeremiah then looks at me in awe and amazed at the power that I had just exuded and admirably shakes my hand, happily knowing that he was going to sleep in his own bed tonight.

Chapter 7

More than ninety percent of the Baltimore murder victims are black. Most of the killings are drug or gang related, but not all of them are. I can remember hearing about the story of the mother who was shot to death in front of her children last June in retaliation for dating a woman's ex-boyfriend, and then there was the 97-year old man who was found shot to death in his home in East Baltimore back in July. Then, of course, what surprised us all in the legal community was when the younger brother of the Baltimore police department's chief spokesman was shot dead for no apparent reason.

The first time I had ever tried a murder case was my first year as a public defender. It apparently was a drug deal gone bad. The suspect shot his victim because the victim shortchanged him on his money. It was $100. $100 was what was in between someone living or dying. At first the case was very overwhelming for me because I knew that someone's life was in my hands. So, depending on how well or how poor I did, this person could spend the rest of his life in jail. Actually, that wasn't what had really worried me though. What had worried me at the time was that if I did lose the case, would this guy's friends or associates try to retaliate against me or my family although I had done the best that I could. Well I eventually did lose that case, and that guy ended up getting 45 years in prison. Now with hundreds of murders that had happened throughout the years, I have handled so many capital murders cases that it just comes second nature to me now.

State of Maryland versus Rodney Whinebeck was the thick capital murder file sprawled out on my desk. I had been working on this case for the past six months and the trial was now starting next week.

This murder was a brazen, assassination style hit done in the middle of the day last September on Labor Day. When the police identified their potential suspect, it was very carelessly handled, and their evidence was very weak and sloppy. Whinebeck had always stated that it wasn't him although he was known to associate with a very violent gang, so the prosecution is doing everything in their power to prove that it was him. The best deal they had offered was 30 years with the possibility of parole after having done 15 years in prison.

Jury selection starts on Monday and the case is scheduled to last for three days. I sit at my desk going through the folder as the music of Thelonious Monk encapsulates the room. I then take a look at the witness lists to see who the prosecution will call on and then look at the list of witnesses that I may plan to call to the stand and make sure that they all had received their subpoenas to come to court on the scheduled days. I then contact my client's family to make sure that they deliver a suit to the jail so that my client could wear it for his trial.

While going through the folder I come across the photos of the victim's dead body sprawled out in the middle of a sidewalk in a neighborhood in West Baltimore. I look very intensely at the face of the victim. A bullet hole was directly over the victim's right eye and his eyes were still wide open. You can still see the fright in the man's eyes. Another picture showed the victim's white tee shirt ripped and bullet riddled, now a dark red from the four bullets that had penetrated through his chest. It amazed me that this guy was only 20 years old.

I can remember when I was only 20 years old and remembered that I was a sophomore in college where my only thoughts were studying my classes, partying, and how to get laid with college girls. Death never crossed my mind.

As I was in a daydream-like state, enthralled over the images of the victim, I didn't notice that Fletcher was standing at my doorway wanting to talk to me.

"Hey Richard, you got a moment?" asked Fletcher.

I snap out of my trance and gaze up at Fletcher. "What's going on, Fletcher?" I asked.

"I see that you are looking at the Whinebeck case. What's your aim on it?" asked Fletcher.

"My client is emphatic that he did not do it. He wants to take his chance at trial no matter what they offered." I say to him.

"What did the state offer?" asked Fletcher.

"30 with parole after 15" I say.

"Ok, let's see what their next offer will be. I'm very sure that they will come back with 20, parole after 10, but keep me informed if you can." stated Fletcher as he turns his back and walks out of my office.

"Alright, will do." I say under my breath.

When I closed the case file, I sit back in my chair and close my eyes while visualizing the crime scene and scenario in my head.

I envision the two young black men standing at the 2400 block of West Pratt Street enthralled in a heated argument. One man is wearing a white tee shirt, faded blue jeans with dingy looking New Balance tennis shoes, and the other man is wearing a black hoody sweatshirt, with a New York Yankees baseball cap underneath the hood, dark blue jeans with dark brown Timberland boots.

I then visualize the suspect pulling out a handgun out of the waistband of his dark jeans and then shooting the victim four times in the chest. As the victim stumbles back and drops to his knees in agony, the suspect then shoots once more, a bullet into the victim's head at pointblank range. The victim then falls back, sprawled halfway onto the sidewalk and on the street, as the suspect then runs down the street and then into an alley way.

The interesting thing is that West Pratt Street is a very busy road, it's a main pipeline into the city, however, I'm really surprised to see that the prosecution only has one eyewitness. Maybe that happened because either this event just so happened to take place during a desolate time in the day, or there were actually many other eyewitnesses however they are too scared and apprehensive to come forward. So, the only actual view of the assailant is a vague description from their eyewitness and a low-resolution video which is produced by a city camera that is affixed to the light post in which the city government places only in certain low-income neighborhoods which are very noticeable by the bright blue flashing lights atop of them.

In the statement that the eyewitness gave, he described the assailant as; between 5'7 – 5'10", medium brown complexion, and a medium build between 180 – 200 pounds, which pretty much describes just about 90 percent of all the black men in Baltimore City. The witness, however, could not clearly see the face of the man because of the baseball cap and hoody the man was wearing. When the eyewitness was shown the street video of the incident along with various mug shots, he identified the suspect.

I do realize that this weak identification is good for us as the defense because since the burden of proof is on the State all I would have to do is just put enough doubt in the jury's head in order to get a 'Not Guilty' verdict.

I then look at my court docket calendar and notice that voir dire starts at 9:00am on Monday. This is where the judge and the attorneys for both sides ask potential jurors questions to determine if they are competent and suitable to serve in the case.

I take this very seriously because errors during jury selection are common grounds for an appeal in many criminal cases such as this. Causes for appeals usually happens when a party is forced to use its limited peremptory challenges on jurors that the court should have stricken for cause because there is a reasonable doubt about their qualifications to serve, so in order to prevent these cases, I am very cautious and careful when I question potential jurors.

I look at my watch and notice that it is 4:30 pm and decide to shut everything down in order to leave the office early for the day. Not only will next week be a very strenuous week for me this weekend will be as well. This is the weekend of Saundra's firm's big fundraising event, so I realize that I will need all the stamina and mental strength that I can get in order to get through a gathering of a bunch of pompous and pretentious individuals. Looking up towards the heavens I state, "God give me strength."

Chapter 8

Each year for the past five years, Saundra and I attend a family friendly fundraising event sponsored by her firm, Scranton Beckford & McCoy which is always held on the third Sunday in March. Usually it's held at one of the lead attorneys' house. This year it is at Kyle Page's home in Bethesda, Maryland. He has a very large home sprawled out on five acres of land which is as grandiose as his personality. Saundra longs for the day when she would be able to host this event one year; however, she feels that we would have to move into a bigger house in the county since she says that she wouldn't feel comfortable hosting it in our current townhouse in Baltimore City. Not that anything is wrong with our house or neighborhood, but she would like to host when we get into a house at least twice the size that we are living in now.

Actually, truth be told, I never really liked attending this event even though it is to help raise money in order to stop human trafficking. It just seems like a bunch of pompous, pretentious people getting together to show off how much money that they can spend.

The event was first initiated by the head partner, Phil Scranton and usually has nearly 200 people attending, all from different walks of life, but mainly lawyers, lobbyists, and politicians with their spouses and children. Phil was never directly affected by human trafficking nor had he ever known of anyone who was trafficked, however, one day he decided that he wanted to "give back" to society so he started a fundraising event. In all actuality though, it's believed that he just picked a hot topic and is doing it mainly for political gain. He is a man known for his tough, aggressive, tactless ways of doing things, not for his humanity.

Although this event is a semi-formal affair, children are allowed to wear clothes that they can play in, so Ciana wears a pair of jeans and a very pretty blue blouse, however, I just wear one of my many black pin-striped suits whereas Saundra wears an elegant, beautifully laced, form-fitting, peach colored dress which highlights her very toned and shapely body, her beautiful brown complexion, and her long wavy black hair.

We reached Kyle's house at ten minutes after eight, however, even though the event started at 7:30 there are literally nearly twenty cars already here which makes finding a parking spot a challenge. A hired parking attendant appears out of the shadows and beckons for me to park the vehicle in an open spot located away from the circular driveway onto a patch of grass next to a few other vehicles.

When we walk to the front door to go inside, the door is opened up by a young freckled face teenaged girl wearing a very pretty white dress with dazzling white buttons. Saundra recognized her from the Christmas party last year, as Kyle's 16-year-old daughter, Cassey, who is volunteering to help guide the guests as they arrive.

"Hi, you must be Cassey, we are the Clayton's" Saundra says emphatically. "I remember you from the Christmas party. How have you been?"

"I'm doing well, thank you. How are you all doing? May I take your coats?" Cassey replies.

"We are doing great. Thanks for asking. Yes, you may, pretty little lady," I say with my debonair charismatic smile.

Cassey then takes our coats and drapes it over her left arm and with her right-hand grabs hold of Ciana's hand to take her to where the other children are playing. Kyle then walks towards me and Saundra and reaches out his hand for me to shake.

The front foyer had a very grandiose, ostentatious appearance to it, with the white marble floor cascading into the double semi-circular staircases which encompasses a huge crystal chandelier hanging from the center of the cathedral ceiling.

"Welcome to my humble abode," Kyle states with a smile.

"Abode? Yes. Humble? The jury is still out on that one," I say laughing as I shake Kyle's hand.

Then Kyle reaches over to give Saundra a hug. "Welcome," he states.

"Your house is lovely, Kyle. So, is Phil here yet? You know I have to be seen if I want more green," laughs Saundra.

"He's in the study talking to a congressman from Pennsylvania. I'll take you there. You know Phil, always trying to get something," replies Kyle.

"That's true, but aren't we all? I want partnership, why else would I be here?" Saundra stating slyly as she and Kyle head for the study leaving me in the midst.

As I stand here a bit bewildered seeing that both my daughter and my wife have left my side, I decide to make a straight beeline for the food table which hosts a wide variety of hors d'oeuvres and a few other tasty looking delicatessens, a bit surprised that there isn't anyone else circling around the table since I always believed that if you want a lawyer to attend an event you better make sure you provide free food.

While standing by the food table, I am approached by Saundra's co-worker, James King. A very tall, nice looking man, James is the only African American male attorney in the firm. A firm that has nearly 40 attorneys and roughly 60 support staff, African Americans make up less than ten percent of the firm. This nearly ten percent include, only four attorneys, one paralegal, two secretaries, and of course, two guys in the mailroom.

James stretches out his hand to introduce himself by shaking my hand.

"You must be Saundra's husband," states James.

"That's right, I'm Richard. How did you guess that I was Saundra's husband?" I ask.

"Uh, well in case you couldn't tell, "we" don't make up large numbers around here," James states as he points to the back of his hand. "I figured that since the other two Black attorneys are not here yet and I really don't think that "THEY" are "down wit' brown", if you know what I mean, you must be with Saundra since I saw her here a few minutes ago. See, it was a bit of a process of elimination here. I'm James, by the way."

"Hey James, good to meet you. What do you practice at the firm?" I asked while stuffing my face with a cream cheese & prosciutto cocktail bite.

"I'm new to the firm. I started here about four weeks ago in the litigation division." He stated.

"Ah, yes! Saundra told me about that position when it was open. She wanted me to go for it." I tell him.

"Oh, you're an attorney as well?" asked James.

"Yes, I'm a criminal defense attorney. I work as a public defender in Baltimore City." I mention.

"Oh cool! How do you like doing that?"

"It's my passion and purpose," I tell him.

"That's great! I thought about going into criminal defense sometime in the future after I rake in the money from corporate first, however, it would most likely be private practice though. I don't think that I could do the PD thing, but I do commend you for your desire to do so." states James.

"Well you know what they say; there are two types of people who become public defenders: those who believe they can save the world and those who know damn well they can't. The former are those starry eyed law school grads convinced that they can make a difference. The latter are those who have worked in the system and know the problems are so much bigger than they are. I guess I'm one of the few unicorns who after all these years, still think that I can make a difference." I say.

Kyle comes to approach us as I am talking.

"That's right Richard, Saundra tells us that you are a Public Defender in Baltimore City. How do you like doing that? Don't you get upset sometimes seeing so many Black males going in and out through the system all the time?" asked Kyle.

James and I are so shocked at the audacity of that statement that we stare at Kyle in unbelief for a few seconds without saying a word and then we look at each other as if we could read each other's mind as if to say, 'Can you believe this mother fucker??'

"Well maybe if the clause in the 13th Amendment which states that slavery is permitted as a punishment for crime, wasn't in there, maybe, just maybe, African-American males wouldn't do hard time for things that their White counterparts are getting away with." I reply.

Kyle gave a very sly smile and then immediately changed the topic. "Saundra is one of our best attorneys. She is a super aggressive litigator. She's like a Pitbull."

"Well Kyle, do you know what the difference is between a female lawyer and a Pitbull?" I ask.

"No, what?" asked Kyle

"Lipstick." I say with a chuckle as I move towards Saundra seeing that she is walking towards me.

"Hey Honey, how was your chat with Phil?" I ask her.

"Uh, you know...same ole' same ole'. I'm just glad that I made myself seen." stated Saundra. "I see that you met James. He's pretty fresh in the field, just passed the bar this past November and he fits in with us like a glove. He has taken the position that I was recommending you for."

"Yeah, I figured that out as he and I were talking. He's a pretty decent guy. Well if it wasn't me at least they did hire another Black guy." I say. "Sooo, how long did you say that we needed to stay?"

"Chill Richard, we've only been here for an hour, the night is still young." replied Saundra.

"Well if I have to spend any more time speaking to Kyle, I think I'll snap."

"Yeah, Kyle can be an arrogant little prick sometimes, but he is a tough litigator and one of the best attorneys at the firm. Anyway, not everyone here is like Kyle. Go mingle, honey, maybe you can make some connections that you so desire for in the political arena." stated Saundra.

"Alright, but let's see if we can leave here no later than 11:00 pm. I've got a big case in the morning."

"Alright, we'll try." She stated.

Chapter 9

I reach the courthouse at 9:12 am, already late for the 9:00 am jury selection process. My day started out late because I had overslept nearly 45 minutes later than anticipated. We didn't reach home last night until after midnight from the fundraising event at Kyle Page's house. Saundra was lucky because her firm allowed anyone who attended the event to take off the next day, with full pay and everything! So of course, Saundra took advantage of the opportunity and stayed home and allowed Ciana to stay home from school as well.

I was hoping that the presiding judge would be late as well although I realize that Judge McHenry is usually a stickler for promptness. I race up the steps instead of using the elevator realizing that waiting for the elevator will probably add another 8 minutes or so to my already late time. When I reach the fourth floor I run to the courtroom and push open the doors. The doors fly open as I enter the courtroom already seeing that the prosecutor, Maxine Stine, is patiently sitting at the prosecution table. The clerk then knocks on a door to inform the bailiff that the defense attorney has arrived and to now bring the defendant into the courtroom.

The defendant, Rodney Whinebeck walks in wearing a cheap looking gray suit which is clearly about two sizes too big for him. His shirt is a light color blue with a dark blue colored clip-on tie that seems to reveal itself every time he turns his head to look back at the people in the pews.

The randomly selected group of 50 people or so sitting in the courtroom pews are the first round of potential jurors waiting to go through the selection process. There will be at least two more sets of fifty in order to find the twelve jurors and three alternates to serve on this case.

The clerk then goes into the judge's chambers and comes back out about five minutes later. There is a knock at a door behind the bench as Judge McHenry then comes walking through the door. The clerk shouts; "All rise!" Everyone then raises as the judge enters the courtroom from his chambers and sits at his bench.

Judge McHenry begins voir dire by asking the prospective jurors questions to ensure that they are legally qualified to serve on a jury and to determine whether jury service would not cause them undue hardship. He then weeds out potential jurors by asking various questions starting with if there are any students who might miss critical exams if they served as a juror, and then asked if anyone has any upcoming surgery scheduled, and if anyone who serves as sole caretaker of an ill or elderly family member who needs to be excused from jury service for undue hardship. Although the judge had only asked about twenty or thirty questions it seemed to be at least one hundred since it took well over an hour to complete his questioning and having to wait for the jurors' response and the clerk having to write down each discrepancy and to dismiss disqualified jurors.

Judge McHenry, Maxine, and I then go into a conference room adjacent to the courtroom and call each remaining potential juror into the room one at a time for questioning. It is now the attorney's turn to ask the potential jurors various questions. My aim is to have jurors who are liberal, understanding, preferably younger, and of course, possibly ethnic. However, the prosecution usually looks for the more conservative, hard nose, older crowd.

If I or the prosecutor believe that there is information which suggests a juror is prejudiced about the case, we can ask the judge to dismiss that juror for cause. For example, a juror can be dismissed for cause if he or she is a close relative of one of the parties or one of the lawyers, or if he or she works for a company that the victim or defendant might have worked for. Each of us may request the dismissal of an unlimited number of jurors for cause. Each request will be considered by the judge and may or may not be allowed.

In addition to challenges for cause, each of us has a specific number of peremptory challenges. These challenges permit a lawyer to excuse a potential juror without stating a cause. In effect, they allow a lawyer to dismiss a juror because of a belief that the juror will not serve in the best interests of the client. Peremptory challenges are limited to a certain number determined by the kind of case being tried, but they just can't be used to discriminate on the basis of race or sex, however, oftentimes they are used for that purpose.

One by one each potential juror steps into the conference room and sits at the head of the long table as Judge McHenry sits directly at the other end, and Me and Maxine are sitting on the sides directly across from one another. Rodney sits next to me with a pen he is twirling around his fingers and a legal yellow pad directly in front of him for writing down any questions that he may have in order to give to me so that I could ask the juror.

The first juror, a middle-aged African American male, comes into the conference room and sits down; definitely looking disinterested and dissatisfied at having to be there. His demeanor was so noticeable that I tried hard not to focus on it in order to not prejudge my decision-making process.

"Juror number one, what do you do for a living?" asked Maxine.

"Construction." stated the man.

"Do you work every day or is it seasonal?" asked Maxine.

"I work every day when the weather is nice." said the man.

"So, are you telling us that if the weather is not nice, you don't work?" asked Maxine.

"That's right." Stated the man.

"How far did you go with your education?"

"I dropped out in the 10th grade but got my GED a year afterwards." Stated the man.

"Do you believe that a person is innocent until proven guilty in a murder trial?" asked Maxine.

"I suppose. I guess it all depends on who was murdered. If it was someone that I knew I may not feel that way."

I didn't feel the need to ask the man any questions because I already made up my mind that I didn't want to use him, and I knew that Maxine probably wasn't going to use him either, so in order to speed up the process of going through 150 potential jurors I learned early on how to minimize this dreadful questioning process.

As juror number two came into the conference room, I noticed that the young man who seemed to be in his twenties seemed to be more interested in staring at Maxine than the questions that was being asked.

When Maxine had finished her questioning and I was to begin mine, I had to say good morning to him twice because the man seemed to be very fixated and enamored with Maxine.

"Good morning sir, how are you? I asked.

"Good morning, I'm good." Stated Juror Number 2.

"Do you feel that there might be any reasons why you may not be able to be fair and judgment free in this case?" I asked.

"Well actually, yes. She's so gorgeous that I will probably just go with whatever way she goes." He states as he points to Maxine.

Judge McHenry and Maxine chuckles as I keep a very straight face realizing that there was no need to ask the man any more questions and to move on.

After almost two hours, Maxine had already gotten three potential jurors to sit on the jury pool, it wasn't until after going through nearly forty jurors, when I finally found a juror that I liked and requested her for the juror pool.

It was an elderly African American woman who reminded me of Jeremiah's grandmother. These types of jurors are always good for the defense because usually they believe that their grandchildren can never do anything wrong.

It took nearly five hours to select all twelve jurors and three alternates for the jury box. It was a very long and tedious process which ended up with seven women and five men. Because it was already after 4:30 in the afternoon, Judge McHenry decided to dismiss for the day and start with opening statements bright and early tomorrow morning. Luckily, I had all my belongings with me and didn't have to go back to the office because I was just too exhausted. I knew that if I went back into the office something would come up and delay me from going home for another hour or two, so I'm going to take my things and just head straight on home.

Chapter 10

Today I was able to reach the courtroom much earlier than I did yesterday. At 8:30 a.m. this morning there were already spectators lining up in front of the courtroom door trying to get in the courtroom to view the case. From the looks of it, spectators for the defense was here as well as for the victim. There is an older woman probably in her 50s being consoled by several people. I even noticed that the prosecutor went over and made a warm gesture to the woman by shaking her hand and placing her other hand on the woman's shoulder. I assume that this woman must be the victim's mother. The woman was surrounded by younger people who resembled her as well as the victim who I thought to be her other children.

The spectators for the defendant were also standing there waiting to get into the courtroom. Ironically, every last one of them seemed to have a pissed, irritated look on their faces. It was almost as if they thought that this was all a big waste of time and the system is just trying to set up yet another innocent Black man.

When I go into the courtroom and sit down at the defense table, the bailiff retrieves Rodney from the back room from where the correctional officers had brought him in from the jail. Rodney is wearing the same oversized suit that he wore into court the day before which is no surprise since the jail will only allow for one suit to be brought in for court.

As Rodney enters, he looks at an area in the courtroom where his family and friends sit and give them a big smile and a head nod acknowledging them there. He then sits to the left of me at the defense table while I place a pen and notepad down in front of him and then start to brief him about what will happen.

After what seemed like an eternity but was actually only about twenty-five minutes, Judge McHenry enters the courtroom to sit on his bench.

"All Rise!" yelled the clerk.

Everyone in the courtroom stands to their feet as the judge approaches his bench.

"Are we ready to get started?" asked Judge McHenry to both me and Maxine.

"Yes, your honor, the Defense is ready." I state.

"The state is ready as well." replied Maxine.

"Very well, we'll get started" stated Judge McHenry as he motions to the clerk to bring in the jury.

The clerk opens the side door which is connected to the jury room where the jurors are sequestered and beckons them to come into the courtroom.

"All rise for the Jury!" the clerk yells.

Everyone in the courtroom including Judge McHenry stands to their feet while the jurors walk in, one by one to take their seats in the jury box.

"Good morning jurors! Is everyone comfortable?" asked Judge McHenry.

The jurors say good morning and nodded unenthusiastically.

"Now I do realize that this is probably not the best way to spend your day, here with me in a courtroom, so I do appreciate you all for coming here and helping with this case." Judge McHenry stated. "Now I would like to explain that you must make a decision based on the notion that it is beyond a reasonable doubt."

That 'beyond a reasonable doubt' clause is not just an afterthought; it is the core of the criminal justice system. A juror can't just think someone might be guilty, the juror isn't supposed to judge a case on his or her emotions – the evidence must be strong enough to remove reasonable doubt from the juror's mind.

"Now, what does that mean?" continued Judge McHenry. "It means that you all must have absolutely no doubt as to the defendant's guilt. The term connotes that the evidence establishes a particular point to a moral certainty and that it is beyond dispute that any reasonable alternative is possible. It does not mean that no doubt exists as to the defendant's guilt, but only that no reasonable doubt is possible from the evidence presented. Do you all understand?"

Some of the jurors nod their heads understanding what the judge had told them, however, a few of the jurors just stare blankly at the judge looking perplexed.

"Ok, I see that some of you still do not understand. Well, let me give you an example. How many of you drove your car here today? Think about yourself and where you parked your car before leaving it to come here. Let's assume that when you parked your car and got out, you noticed that the mileage on it was 5000 miles. You think nothing of it and then you come inside to the courthouse. You are here all day long and then when we finish and close for the day you go back to your car and it is in the same spot where you left it and the miles on the odometer still says 5000. Would you have a reasonable doubt as to whether your car was there all day? Probably not. Now, the reality is that your car might not have been there all day parked in that space. Your car might have been on a flatbed pick-up truck going up and down the highway. It is possible that someone could have picked up your car, driven it around on a truck and then returned it in the same location before you came back to the vehicle. Now, it is possible that that could have happened but is it reasonable to believe that could have happened? Most people would say no. Now let's suppose that when you left the courthouse and went to your car, there was a police officer there who asked you if you were the owner of this car, and states that he witnessed a man with a flatbed truck pick up your car and drove with it around the city and then dropped it back off here. Now assuming that you believe the officer, would you now have a reasonable doubt as to whether your car was there or not? Most people would say yes. So, you see, a reasonable doubt comes from the evidence, the facts that you have, the lack of evidence, and things like that. So, you, the jury will hear the evidence of the case or lack thereof, and will discuss the doubts when you go back to the jury room and then decide whether those doubts are reasonable and together as a jury you will come up with a conclusion whether the case has been proven beyond a reasonable doubt."

The jury listened to the judge intensely and seemed to have a better understanding of what Judge McHenry was saying.

"Do you all understand now?" asked Judge McHenry?

All the members of the jury now nod their heads in acknowledgement.

"Good. Are there any questions, comments, or concerns from anyone here?" asked Judge McHenry.

I look at Rodney who is just staring down doodling on the pad that I had placed in front of him, then turn to the judge and state; "The Defense has none."

"The State has none either," stated Maxine.

"Ok, then let's proceed with this case." stated Judge McHenry.

Just then, the clerk stood up and read the case title and the defendant's charge.

"State of Maryland versus Rodney Whinebeck, docket number 032975. State of Maryland, criminal circuit court of Baltimore City, March 14, 2017. The grand jurors of the State of Maryland duly selected a panel sworn and charged to acquire for the city of Baltimore, Maryland, upon their oath present that Rodney Whinebeck, on September 5, 2016, in Baltimore City, and before the finding of this indictment, did unlawfully, intentionally, willfully, and with premeditation, intend to kill Jerry Smith in violation of Maryland Criminal Law Code, Section 2-201; Murder in the First Degree. This indictment is signed by the Maryland District Attorney."

"How does the Defendant plea to this indictment?" asked Judge McHenry.

I stand up and say, "Not Guilty."

"Ok, we will now begin the opening statements. Ms. Stine, could you please start your opening statement?" asked Judge McHenry.

"Yes, your Honor," she states as she gets up and walks toward the front of the jury box.

"Good morning Jurors." Maxine says as she slowly and methodically speaks to the jurors making sure she looks at each and every one of them straight in the eye as she speaks. "On Labor Day, September 5, 2016,

Jerry Smith was going to see his friends and family at a cookout that his sister was hosting celebrating the holiday and the fact that he had just started a new job as a construction worker for Browns and Meddow Constructors the week before. As he was walking to his sister's house after getting off the number 12 bus, a man approached him and started an argument with him. Jerry started to argue back with the man to defend whatever accusations the man was implying. Without warning he was horrifically, brutally shot 5 times…, four bullets in the chest and one bullet to the head, …and was left for dead three blocks away from his sister's house on the 2400 block of West Pratt Street here in Baltimore City. Shot and killed by a ruthless, and heartless assailant wearing dark blue jeans and a black hooded sweatshirt. Through a very thorough investigation done by Baltimore City Police Department, the assailant was identified as the man sitting right there at the defense table, Mr. Rodney Whinebeck. During this case, the State will prove beyond a reasonable doubt that the defendant, Rodney Whinebeck, was that assailant who had brutally murdered Jerry Smith in a senseless act of rage and murder for hire. We will prove that Mr. Whinebeck is affiliated with the gang, the "9th Street Killas" in which they had contracted him out and orchestrated the calculated hit on Jerry Smith. The Defense will try to manipulate your minds and try to put up a smoke screen to try to make you doubt the facts, but let it be clear that the facts are the facts. Whether you try to bend or stretch the truth the facts remain the facts. I ask that you listen very carefully to the facts and know the truth that Mr. Rodney Whinebeck is a ruthless diabolical killer who needs to be taken off the streets of Baltimore and locked up for the rest of his natural life."

Maxine turns back to her table to sit down as I now get up and approach the jury. I try to read the expression on the jurors faces in the hopes of identifying the more outspoken juror, knowing that this person would probably be the one who will influence the others with their decision, however, I'm unable to identify that person this early in the game.

"Ladies and gentlemen of the jury, I want you to take a good long look at Mr. Rodney Whinebeck. Look at his facial features. Look at his skin complexion. Look at his size, and even closely look at his face and the mole on the right side of his cheek. The State is trying to put a square peg in a round hole. They have such a vague description of the assailant that it could be 90 percent of all the Black men here in Baltimore City. I'm sure that every one of you knows at least one person who would fit the description that they are saying. The State says to pay attention to the facts. I actually agree with her on that. When they present the video, I want you to look very hard and long at it. Watch it over and over again. Look at the facts as to who that person in the video may be, then look at Mr. Whinebeck. Not only look for the similarities but also look at the differences. You all are here to provide justice, not to become a vigilante on an innocent man. The State's mindset is, 'Hey, at least we got somebody! He might not have done this crime but look at him, I'm sure he did something wrong.' They are going to paint him out to be this ruthless sociopath who has an extensive record. Yes,

Mr. Whinebeck does have a criminal record, but he is not a murderer. So what, that he has more than a few misdemeanors on his record. This is a man that despite his past, he had changed his life and became a productive individual in society. A man who lives with his elderly grandmother in order to take care of her. A man who has a relationship with his kids. A man who helps anyone in his neighborhood who needs help. Again, listen to the facts and look at all the details. Rodney Whinebeck is a productive innocent man."

I pause for about a minute looking over the jury one person at a time then I turn to return to my seat at the defense table.

"State, call your first witness," Judge McHenry exclaims.

"The State will call Robert Hench as their first witness," stated Maxine.

The bailiff then goes out of the courtroom door in order to retrieve Robert Hench from the hallway to testify. A big, rotund white male comes into the courtroom behind the bailiff and just before he goes to sit in the chair at the witness stand, the bailiff has him raise his right hand in order to be sworn in under oath.

"Do you swear that the testimony that you are about to give shall be the truth, the whole truth, and nothing but the truth, so help you God?"

"Yes, I do." Stated Robert Hench.

"Good morning, Mr. Hench. Could you please state your name and city of residence for the record?" asked Maxine.

"Good morning, my name is Robert Hench, that's H-E-N-C-H, most people just call me Bob. I live in

Baltimore City, Maryland."

"Ok Bob, well could you tell me what you saw on September 5, 2016 at approximately 2:15 pm at the 2400 block of West Pratt Street in Baltimore?"

"Sure. Well as I was driving back to the office while I was on my way back from fixing a customer's HVAC furnish system, I saw a man run up to another man on the sidewalk and start yelling at him. The other man started to yell back and then I saw the man who started the confrontation pull out a gun from his waist and shoot the other man in the chest and then in the head. Afterwards the man ran up the street and disappeared into an alley."

"The man who you saw with the gun, describe for us how he looked."

"Well, he was a black guy, and from where I was, he looked like he was about five foot eight or nine. He had a black sweater with a hood covering his head although it was eighty degrees outside." explained Bob.

"Does he look like the Defendant?" asked Maxine.

"Yes ma'am, that looks like the man." replied Bob.

"How far away were you from the incident?" asked Maxine.

"Oh, I'd say about maybe 300 or 400 feet or so. I was a block away"

"What did you do after you saw the incident?"

"Well I pulled out my cell phone and dialed 911."

"Were you still driving when all this happened?"

"No, I was stopped at a red light when all of it went down."

"Were there any other cars around you when all of this was going down?"

"Yes, I believe that there was a car next to me, however, during the incident the car turned onto the street at the right and sped off."

"Did anyone coerce your testimony or statements?"

"No, I am doing this on my own accord."

"Thank you. No further questions," Maxine stated to the Judge.

"Ok, Defense may cross-examine the witness." stated Judge McHenry.

I get up confidently and walk towards the witness bench where Bob is sitting.

"Hello Bob, let me ask you, how are you SO sure that it was the Defendant, Rodney Whinebeck, sitting at my table who is the actual assailant?" I ask.

"I have pretty good vision. When I saw him charging at the other man, I figured that he might be up to no good, so I was watching very hard." He states.

"How can you actually be 100 percent sure when you had just stated in your testimony that he was 300 or 400 feet away from you even knowing the fact that the assailant wore a baseball cap and a hooded sweatshirt over his head?" I ask.

"Well, I feel as though I have a pretty good memory with faces, so I think that I would remember his face." replied Bob.

"You stated that you were coming back from fixing a customer's HVAC system. Is that correct?"

"Yes sir. That is correct."

"How many customers did you have that day?"

"Oh, I'd say about 4."

"Can you describe the appearance of the customer you serviced right before this incident happened?"

"No, I cannot. I wasn't focused on him. When I go to a customer's place, I speak with them very briefly and then I focus on the machine. If I am there for an hour, I may only look at the customers for about 3 to 5 minutes the entire time."

"Ok, fair enough. Did you work yesterday?"

"Yes, I did."

"Can you describe for me the customer you met yesterday?"

"Unfortunately, I cannot. Again, I did not focus on them."

"Let me make sure that I understand what you are saying correctly. You cannot even remember the last customer you had even yesterday because you did not focus on that person, yet you can remember the defendant because you focused on him even though you were not 100 feet, not 200 feet, but 300 to 400 feet away? 300 feet is about from where you sitting right now to the bench on the other side of the hallway outside this courtroom, yet you can see him very clearly even though his face was obstructed"

"Well I did try to focus on him when he was doing the shooting."

"Oh ok, well what color was the New York Yankees baseball cap he was wearing? Blue or black?"

"I couldn't really tell from that distance."

"Oh, I see, so from that distance you could not tell if the baseball cap was either blue or black however you could tell that the defendant was the assailant even though his face was partially obscured?" I ask.

"Yes, I do believe that it was him." Bob stated obviously getting annoyed.

"Bob, you stated that you were stopped at a red light when the arguing with the two men begun. Why didn't you pull out your cell phone and start video recording the incident since you suspected that something was about to happen?"

"Everything happened so fast. I just didn't think about it at the time."

"But you were witnessing a brutal murder, I don't understand why you didn't try to get an accurate picture using your phone knowing that you could use a telephoto lens to get a closer view?"

"Again, I just didn't think about it at the time." stated Bob.

"No further questions." I then turn to the jury and say, "Ladies and gentlemen of the jury, please be aware that his description of the assailant is very weak and sketchy. Realize that you could be sending an innocent man to prison."

When I go back to take my seat at the defense table, I notice the different expressions on the observers faces who are sitting in the courtroom. Those who are for the defendant looked jubilated, however, those who are for the prosecutor look very disturbed. Yet the faces of the jurors were stoned-faced with absolutely no expression, so it was very difficult for me to get an accurate read on any of the jurors.

"Call your next witness." Judge McHenry says to Maxine.

"The state now calls Detective Barry Collars to the stand." proclaims Maxine.

The tall astute blond-headed man who comes walking into the courtroom approached the witness stand with his right hand already raised waiting for the clerk to swear him in.

"Good morning Detective, could you please state your name and your occupation for the record?" asked Maxine.

"Yes, my name is Detective Barry Collars and I am a detective with Baltimore City Police Department, Homicide Division."

"Detective, how were you assigned this case?"

"Normally homicide cases are assigned on a revolving basis to about twenty different homicide detectives, so we don't usually know what we are going to be assigned until the case comes in. However, with this case, I chose to take it on because I recognized the assailant from the video."

"When did you recognize the assailant?"

"When I viewed the street video, I made out the assailant as Mr. Whinebeck because I had dealt with him before about two months prior to the incident when I was helping a fellow officer with an armed robbery case."

"Was he the suspect in that case?"

"Yes he was."

"What was the outcome of that case?"

"The victim wasn't able to identify him correctly, so we had to release him."

"What happened on September 5, 2016?"

"Well, when I got to the crime scene, I saw a young African American male sprawled out on the sidewalk with multiple gunshot wounds to the torso and one shot to the head. We identified the victim as Jerry Smith through the driver's license we found in his wallet. I noticed that this particular part of the area is monitored by cameras, so I immediately requested the film footage. When I viewed the footage, I immediately recognized the assailant as Rodney Whinebeck. We picked him up the next day at his grandmother's residence."

"Did you question the suspect?"

"Yes we did, however, he chose not to talk until he had legal representation."

"Ok, no further questions."

"Would defense like to cross-examine the witness?" asked Judge McHenry.

"Yes, your Honor, we would." I state.

"Detective Collars, how can you tell that it is Rodney Whinebeck on the video?"

"I recognized him from the last time he had been arrested two months prior."

"You recognized him even though the assailant was wearing a hooded sweatshirt and a baseball cap?"

"Yes, I could just tell. Through my 30 years of experience, I have a very keen sense for identifying people."

"Detective, do all Black men look alike to you?"

"Objection!!" yelled out Maxine.

"Sustain." said Judge McHenry.

"Let me rephrase that question, do most of the African American men who you have arrested have similar characteristics?"

"There are some similarities however they are not identical."

"Detective, isn't it true that when you had to release Mr. Whinebeck on the armed robbery charge two months prior to this incident, you were so upset because the victim failed to identify him correctly that you tried to get him on an entirely different charge?"

"No, however, it is common for us to look at other cases to see if a suspect was involved in any other crimes."

"Isn't it true that you want to solve this case so badly, that you identified Mr. Whinebeck as the assailant because of the similarities between him and the real assailant?"

"No, that is not true at all."

"Detective, when you arrested Mr. Whinebeck did you search the residence where you found him to try and find the gun that was used in the murder?"

"Yes, we did search the residence however we did not find the murder weapon there."

"Did you ever find the murder weapon?"

"No, we did not."

"Where else did you search for it?"

"We searched his car, his girlfriend's apartment, and his cousin's house. These are the other places that he is known to reside at."

"And with no prevail, you did not find the gun, did you?"

"No, we did not."

"Detective, did you run the ballistics on the shell casings?"

"Yes, we did. It showed that the bullet came from a .45."

"A .45 caliber weapon?" I ask to reassure his answer.

"Yes, that is correct."

"Detective, you told the State that cases are assigned to detectives on a revolving basis, is that correct?"

"Yes, that's correct."

"How is that done?"

"Well normally our supervisor would review a homicide report and distribute that case."

"Is your supervisor the Chief?"

"Yes, that's correct."

"So, just so that I can understand, a murder happens, then first responders arrive to the scene to take a report and then it goes to the Chief and then would go to the homicide division and assigned to a detective. Is that correct?"

"Yes, that's correct."

"Okay, now I don't understand. You told the State that you arrived at the crime scene as a first responder. I will quote what you said, 'when I came to the crime scene, I saw a young African-American male sprawled out on the sidewalk with multiple gunshot wounds to the torso and one shot to the head.' How is it that you just happened to be there and then just happened to be assigned this case?"

"I was close to the area when I heard it on the CB radio."

"Okay. Thank you. No further questions."

"The State's witness may step down." stated Judge McHenry. "Does the State have any more witnesses?"

"Yes, Your Honor. The State calls Stanley Henry." proclaimed Maxine.

The Bailiff goes through a door behind the judge's bench and out comes with a middle aged African American man wearing a bright yellow jumpsuit with the words, 'Maryland Department of Corrections' imprinted on the back, approaching the witness stand.

"Please state your name for the record." stated Maxine.

"My name is Stanley Henry."

"Mr. Henry, how do you know Rodney Whinebeck?"

"We both shared a cell together when I was at BCCB. He was my cellie before I got my sentence and was transferred to JCI."

"JCI? So that the jury knows what you are referring to, what does that stand for?" asked Maxine.

"Jessup Correctional Institution."

"Did Mr. Whinebeck tell you anything while you both were sharing a cell?"

"Yes, he told me that he killed Jerry Smith because Jerry was in a rival gang."

"Did you believe him when he told you that?"

"Yes, because he gave a lot of details about the hit."

"What did he say?"

"He told me that he saw Jerry walking on Pratt, so he stepped up to him and then they started to fuss at each other. Rodney then said that he pulled out his Glock 9 and shot him several times."

"Did you believe him when he told you this?"

"Of course, I did. He told me in great detail about who he was and that he has no problem killing anyone."

"Ok, thank you. No further questions."

"Would defense like to cross-examine the witness?"

"Absolutely, Your Honor." I retort.

"Mr. Henry, what are you incarcerated for?"

"Objection, Your Honor. That is irrelevant to the case. Counselor is trying to influence the jury" stated Maxine.

"Your Honor, I need to know whether he has any motive for his testimony." I say.

"Overruled. Witness answer the question." stated Judge McHenry.

"I'm in for rape." stated Stanley.

"How much time are you sentenced to?

"31 years." Stanley stated softly.

"Mr. Henry, isn't it true that you are giving this testimony in the hopes of getting some time off of your sentence?" I ask.

"Well they did tell me that if I help them with this case that they would shed a few years off of my sentence. I see no wrong in getting something by telling the truth. If it helps me see my family sooner, then so be it."

"So, if I'm clear, your motive for helping the State is to shed a few years off your sentence. Fair enough. People will lie and do anything to help themselves." I insinuate sarcastically.

"I'm not lying!!" he yelled.

"Ok. In your testimony, you stated that Mr. Whinebeck told you that he walked up to Jerry, started to fuss with him, and then pulled out his Glock 9 to shoot him multiple times. Is that correct?"

"Yes, that is correct. He told me that word to word."

"So, he pulled out his Glock 9..."

"Yes, that's what he said."

"Did you know, Mr. Henry, that the ballistics that was run on the shell casings and bullets found at the location was determined that the gun was not a nine-millimeter but a .45. Those are two distinctive types of guns. There is no way that anyone could confuse one from the other. No one knew the ballistics except for the police, the prosecution, me, and of course, the true assailant. I believe that you just made up this story just to lower your time. The defense has no further questions."

"Does the defense have any witnesses to present?" asked Judge McHenry.

"Your Honor, we did have two different character witnesses however, one was unable to make it due to a family emergency and although the other person is here, however, we just decided not to use her. However, I would like to play the surveillance video from the street cameras for the jury again though.."

The video plays out for the jury as the entire crime scene takes place. I have the video play twice. The second time it plays I pause it on the point where they could see the front of the suspects face and then zoomed in.

"Take a good look at the assailant on the monitor." I tell the jury.

I then take off my suit jacket hang it on the back of my chair and then reach for the gym bag that was behind my chair. From the bag, I take out a black hoody sweatshirt and put it on, then I take out a New York Yankees baseball cap and put it on my head and put the hoody over my head and the cap, then I face the jury standing right next to the still picture of the assailant on the monitor.

"Can you tell a difference?" I ask the jury. "The Defense rests."

"Will the State now give their closing arguments." Asked Judge McHenry.

Maxine gets up from her table to approach the jury.

"Good afternoon, ladies and gentlemen. Today, I had presented to you three witnesses who could confirm the identity of the assailant to be that of the defendant who violently shot and murdered in cold blood, Jerry Smith.

Jerry Smith was a hardworking young man, just going to see his friends and his family on Labor Day when Rodney Whinebeck came up to him and fatally shot Jerry in the torso four times, and when that wasn't enough, shot him in the head at point blank range to make sure that Jerry was going to be dead.

Mr. Whinebeck has been in trouble since he was 12 years old, constantly in and out of jail. He is a career criminal who would do anything for money and status. You sat right there and watched the video of the brutal murder. You can see who the assailant was in that video. You listened to the eyewitness clearly identify Mr. Whinebeck. You even heard from a man who lived with Mr. Whinebeck day in and day out in a 7 by 10-foot cell for four months and how he told the witness the details of this vicious, heinous crime that he had committed. I ask of you all to do the right thing and put this man away for a very long time so he is unable to take away anyone else's precious life. Thank you."

Maxine then returns to her seat as I get up to approach the jury.

"Ladies and gentlemen of the jury, you all sat here and listened to the testimony of the three witnesses that the State had provided. The State had failed beyond a reasonable doubt to prove that the defendant, Rodney Whinebeck, is guilty. They first brought in an eyewitness who claimed that he was 100% sure that

Mr. Whinebeck was the assailant, yet he couldn't even remember the description of the last customer that he had dealt with just 24 hours ago. When I put on a baseball cap and a hooded sweatshirt, I am sure that he would not have been able to tell the difference between me and my client from a distance of 300 to 400 feet. The State then brought in a detective from the Baltimore City police department who had taken on the case. Detective Collars had actually volunteered to take this particular case because he said that the man in the video looked like the man he arrested a month or two ago who had gotten away with armed robbery. Here he already accused Mr. Whinebeck of "getting away with robbery" and because of his personal vendetta against Mr. Whinebeck, Detective Collars is trying to make sure that he doesn't get away with anything else. Couldn't get him with robbery, why not pin a murder to this man? The Detective even searched in all the locations that my client resides at and yet still did not find the murder weapon. They found absolutely nothing. Not even a trace of anything that would place Mr. Whinebeck at the scene of the crime. Not even the New York Yankees baseball cap. Then, because the State's case is so weak, they bring in a convicted felon of all people, into court as their next witness. Any man who rapes women should be in jail. They should be in jail for a very long time, yet the State promised him to shed some time off of his sentence in lieu of his testimony. That doesn't just sound illegal, it sounds immoral. And to make matters worse, the prosecution brings up Mr. Whinebeck's juvenile record in her closing argument!! Ladies and gentlemen, you must see that the pieces to the puzzle do not fit. The State is trying to make a picture out of pieces that just don't fit, and if the pieces don't fit then you must acquit! Thank you."

I finish and return to my seat.

"Members of the jury, it is now time for you to deliberate in order to come up with a unanimous verdict." Stated Judge McHenry. "If there is a legal question that you need explaining, the one who is chosen as the foreman must write a note and then knock on the door of your room. There will be a clerk sitting on the other side that will retrieve your note and bring it to me. Then the clerk will bring you all out back into this courtroom where I will explain the answer. When you have reached the verdict, again, you will write a note saying that you have reached your verdict and hand it to the clerk outside your door. However, do not write the actual verdict on the slip. Then the clerk will bring you back into the courtroom where at that time you will hand me the slip with the verdict on it. Do you all understand?" asked Judge McHenry.

The jury all stated 'yes' as the clerk got up to approach the jury.

"All Rise for the Jury." yelled the clerk.

Everyone in the courtroom once again stands up as the jury was led out of the courtroom into the secluded back jury room.

Rodney was then handcuffed and returned back to the holding cell by the correctional officers who were sitting behind him in the courtroom. I decided to head back to my office until the verdict was reached.

When I got back to my office I wanted to keep my mind off of the case and just chill and relax with my feet elevated on the desk listening to classical music.

After three hours of deliberations, I had gotten the call that the jury had finally reached its verdict. I headed back to the courtroom and waited for the jury to come in. The clerk asks the jurors to come back into the courtroom and take their prospective seats. Judge McHenry then asks the jury if they had reached a unanimous decision. The jurors all nod their heads as the foreman of the group stands up and tells the Judge that they have. The foreman then sticks out his hand with the verdict slip in it to hand to the bailiff to give to the judge. Judge McHenry reads the verdict slip and then hands it back to give back to the foreman.

"In the case of the State of Maryland versus Rodney Whinebeck, docket number 032975, for Count One; Murder in the First Degree, how does the jury rule?" the clerk shouts asking the jury.

There was a deadening silence in the courtroom which seemed to last an eternity. I look intently at the foreman trying to get a read on him as if trying to anticipate the answer. The bailiff and the correctional officers step closer to Rodney just in case he flips out and does something erratic if he doesn't like what he hears, however Rodney just calmly sits back in his chair instead of standing up as if he's not worried about a thing.

"We the Jury, find the defendant NOT guilty." exclaimed the foreman.

As soon as the verdict was read, the woman who seemed to be the mother of the murder victim dropped down on her knees and cried very loud and hard.

"No!! Nooo!!! Oh Jesus! Oh my Lord!" the woman cried out. "He killed my son and got away with it! He killed my son and GOT AWAY WITH IT!! This isn't right! It's just not fair!"

Judge McHenry ignored the commotion that was going on in the courtroom and continued to instruct the jurors of their parting instructions. As the jurors were released from duty and were walking out of the courtroom in a line, not one of the jurors looked directly at the weeping mother.

I look briefly at the grieving mother and then averted my eyes towards my smiling client. I then extend my hand to give Rodney a handshake and wish him good luck as I gather my belonging to head out of the courtroom as if I was in a rush.

As I swiftly leave the courtroom, I look down toward the ground to assure that I will not make any eye contact with anyone. I don't want to see anyone who might be associated with the victim nor the defendant, knowing that the expression on their faces would tell a story longer than a 400-page novel. The victim's side would have very angry and hurt expressions on their faces and the defense's side would be happy and act as if they would want to be my new best friend. I didn't want any part of any of it, so I hurry my way out of the courtroom and down the steps to reach the exit of the courthouse.

Just as I am about to take a foot outside the courthouse door, I realize that I have forgotten one of my folders under the defense table where I was sitting so of course, I turn around to head back to the stairs in order to go back to the courtroom where I was sitting.

When I reach back on the fourth floor I notice that everyone is finally gone, and it is now very quiet so I am able to take my time and stroll back into the courtroom to pick up the folder that I left behind on the floor under the defense table.

I find the folder and place it back into my briefcase and then decide to take the elevator down instead of the stairs. For whatever reason, the elevator seems to take forever to come but since I'm no longer in a rush, I patiently wait for its arrival.

As the elevator arrives and the doors open, the woman who was in the courtroom crying was in the elevator coming down from an upper floor. I immediately recognized the woman as the mother of the slain victim. I hesitate to step into the elevator, contemplating in my mind as to whether I should go in it or not since this was the woman who I'm sure felt that no justice was done for her son. In her mind, I am sure that she felt that I was just as bad as Rodney Whinebeck. After a moment of thinking, I step into the elevator and push the already lit 'Lobby' button and then stare straight at the elevator doors hoping that the ride would end quickly.

"Have you ever had a child of yours die, Mr. Clayton?" asked the woman in a very soft voice.

"I'm sorry ma'am, did you say something?" I ask as I slightly turn around towards where the woman is standing.

"Yes I did, Mr. Clayton. I said; have you ever had a child of yours die?" repeated the woman.

I hesitate in answering the woman, secretly hoping that the doors of the elevator would hurry up to open so that I could leave before answering the woman.

Realizing that the elevator is taking its own little sweet time to get to my destination, I decide to go ahead and answer the woman.

"Ma'am, I gather you must be the victim Jerry Smith's mother. Look, I am really sorry for your loss and I understand what you must be going through, but I come here to do a job. A job that I am really good at. I help many African Americans get a fair shake in the law where there was always unbalance. Again, I am really sorry for your loss and I do understand your pain, but justice was served. An innocent man is not going to be incarcerated for the rest of his life."

"You didn't answer my question Mr. Clayton. Have you ever had a child of yours die?" asked the woman.

I thought for a moment before answering remembering my wife's two miscarriages but decide not to mention that. "No, I have not!"

"Well I pray to God that you never ever have to go through the pain of losing a child, especially to unnecessary violence, however, you could never understand my pain or know what I have been going through. I know that man was guilty. I know it deep down in my heart that he killed my son. What you are doing is not right, and I hope and pray that one day God will show you your ways."

Just then the doors of the elevator open and the woman walks out as I stand still and dumbfounded.

Chapter 11

After a very long and treacherous week, I am very happy that I am waking up to a beautiful, bright Saturday morning. I plan to spend this beautiful spring day with Saundra and Ciana doing something very special with them. I would like to do some family activity that would bring us even closer together since this past week I unfortunately was so busy that I neglected the both of them and instead was so focused on the Whinebeck trial.

Not sure of what to do and how to spend the day with them, I ask the both of them at breakfast if there was anything that they would like to do on this glorious day.

"Hey, my beautiful Love, what interesting and exciting thing would you like to do today?" I ask Saundra.

"Sweetheart, honestly, what would be exciting to me is for me to just stay home to relax and rest all day. Maybe it could just be a special day with you and Ciana. Truly, I'm just ready to go back to sleep and sleep away the day." She chuckles.

"Aww, Sweetie, I was really hoping that we all could do something as a family today, maybe go somewhere and then come back tomorrow."

"I know, but I am really just very mentally exhausted. Could we plan a family outing at another time, please? We have all the time in the world to enjoy each other, I just want to enjoy my sleep this weekend. Is that okay with you?"

"Sure, I guess so. I'm going to be hurt but I guess one day I will get over it." I say jokingly. "Cianna, I guess it's just you and me. Where would you like to go?"

"I don't know." She says.

"Uhh, I'm not really sure where 'I don't know' is. What state is that place in? Umm, Saundra, do you know where 'I don't know' is?" I ask.

"Dad?!? You know what I mean." Cianna says.

"I'm sorry Cianna, I really don't. Where is 'I don't know' located?"

"Ok, I get it. Ok, well how about we go to the Harbor?" Cianna states.

"The Harbor?   That's not special.   We live downtown, we always walk to the Harbor."

"Yeah, that's true. Well how about we go to the caverns in Virginia?" says Cianna.

"Actually, that is a very good idea! See, I knew you knew where 'I don't know' was. Great, we'll go there and spend the day there then."

"Can we bring Samantha with us?"

"It might be a little too long of a trip for Samantha, so let's just let her keep mommy company." I say. "Now, let's get ready for our trip and try to leave here in about an hour or so."

"Ok, Dad."

"Hey Love, are you sure that you don't want to join us? It will be fun. We could get a hotel room and you can always relax there if you like" I say to Saundra.

"I think I'll go ahead and pass on this one this time. Sleep is calling my name." Saundra says.

"Ok Love, we'll miss you. Hey Ciana, I'll pack some food and supplies for us, would you like me to pack some granola for a snack?"

"Sure." replies Ciana.

The four-hour drive to Luray was laborious but enjoyable. We spent the time talking, singing, and playing visual games such as 'I Spy,' while stopping a few times for restroom breaks.

It seemed to be a very long and desolate drive; however, when we finally reached our destination the beauty of the landscape was majestic. The area was surrounded by trees and mountains as far as the eye could see.

"We're finally here!" I exclaimed. "How do you like it?"

"It's beautiful! Can we go to the caverns now?" asked Ciana.

"Let's first stop by the visitor's desk to get information on everything that's here."

While we were heading to the visitor desk, we walked past a collection of other cool but unrelated attractions — including a ropes course, a hedge maze and a museum of classic cars — in order to find the visitor's desk in which the caverns' entrance was in. It is housed in a building with an architectural style reminiscent of a New Jersey Turnpike rest stop.

"Hi! I'm Gloria. You're just in time. We are about to begin our next tour." A bubbly bright-eyed woman said to us as we stepped into the building.

"Hi." Both me and Ciana say in unison.

"Have you all been out here before?" asked Gloria.

"No, this is our first time." I tell her.

"Great! Then prepare to be amazed! Follow me." Gloria says as she leads us and the group of other tourist through a doorway which led to a small downward staircase.

As the group walked down the stairs, the view widened until we found ourselves at the mouth of an enormous cave, decorated lavishly with curtains and columns of sepia-toned stone.

"Wow!" I exclaimed.

"I know, Dad. This is incredible." Says Ciana.

"Virginia is riddled with underground chambers like this. In fact, there are nearly 4,000 caves in the state, though most are on private property and accessible only to spelunkers with the training and fortitude to wiggle through tiny, dark holes in the ground. We here, on the other hand, are a hit with tourists because our caves are conveniently paved and well lit." explains Gloria. "All 748 of our lights are on timers. I do not want to leave anyone behind in cave darkness. So please stay with the group at all times," She says, with the high-low cadence of a flight attendant giving a safety briefing.

Thus, began our tour of the cave, a leisurely, hour-long walk on a winding path through what was once an ancient sea. When the water drained, it formed caverns that were decorated by the slow drip of water through layers of limestone and clay. Calcite-rich drips from the ceiling become stalactites, drips on the floor accumulated into stalagmites — and when the two met in the middle, they created enormous columns of stone.

"This formation is called Pluto's Ghost, named after the Roman myth of Pluto not Disney's cartoon dog." Gloria says with a smile as she points to a 500-foot pillar towering over them. "You have to remember that when people first explored these caverns, they only had flickering candles or gas lamps, so they thought that they felt the presence of the lord of the underworld was following them."

Many of the cave's rock formations have even more poetic names. Among them is Saracen's Tent, a drapery of nearly paper-thin stone that formed when mineral-bearing water dripped down the ceiling's serrated incline. Then there was the most beautiful sight of the tour: the perfectly still Dream Lake, which reflects the enormous stalactites hanging above, making it look much deeper than it really is.

Near the end of the tour, Gloria guided our group to enter a large, open part of the cave called the Cathedral, where, she explained that in 1954, a man named Leland Sprinkle installed an electric church organ and wired it up to tiny hammers that bang on stalagmites and stalactites to produce different notes. Gloria then pressed a button to make the organ play a Lutheran hymn.

"Isn't this the best rock music you've ever heard?" she asked, a pun that made the group groan.

A short walk later, Gloria guided everyone back to the staircase where we had started. Outside, the air had warmed up more and the sun seemed to be brighter than before.

"How did you like the cavern?" I ask Ciana.

"It was great! It was really unbelievable!" shouts Ciana. "Can we do the Garden Maze next?"

"Of course, we can. We are here to explore everything we can."

We enter the giant maze which is made up of an acre of 8-foot tall evergreen bushes set about in a maze-like formation. One way in and one way out riddled with a bunch of dead ends. After about thirty -

five minutes of wrong turns and dead ends, we realize that this behemoth labyrinth proved to be more difficult to conquer than we thought.

"Dad, I think that I'm ready to get out of here now." Stated Ciana.

"I know, me too."

"Hey look, Dad! There is a platform over there. We could try to stand on it and see if we can look over the bushes to see the exit."

"That's a great idea. Sit on my shoulders while I stand on it and let's see what we can see."

"Ali oop!" I say as I hoist Ciana to my shoulders. "Do you see an exit strategy?"

"Yes, I think so. If we make a right from here and then go left, and then the second right, we should be out."

"Cool beans! Let's get going."

After another ten minutes, Ciana and I finally find our way out of the maze. There were two adjacent buildings that were close to the maze, the toy museum and the car museum. We spent at least another two hours exploring and then headed to the car to wrap up our day-long adventure.

"Did you have a great day today?" I ask.

"It was awesome! Thanks, Dad, for taking me."

"Yeah, it was pretty cool. I'll call your mom and let her know that we're heading back now" I state as Ciana starts to drift off to sleep in the back seat.

I then pick up my cell phone to call Saundra, but it goes directly to voicemail, so I end up leaving a message.

"Hey hon, we are on our way back, I'll try to call you when we're closer." I tell her.

I then immediately call once more just in case the call goes through, but of course once again it goes directly to her voicemail, so I just hang up.

The long treacherous drive back is starting to take a toll on me. From the long hard week to the long trip and all-day excitement that we had is starting to catch up. I wish Saundra just came with us so we could just spend the night at the hotel. Realizing that my eyes are getting heavy I pull over at the next rest stop, buy a large coffee and a small Red Bull. I play the 90s hip hop station on XM, pour the Red Bull into my coffee, and jam until I see the city lights of Baltimore.

Chapter 12

"Ciana…wake up sweetie. We're home now."

"We're home?"

"Yes, we're home now. It's after ten o'clock. You need to get in the house and change your clothes for bed. I have to get Sam and walk her before turning in."

"Can I go with you?"

"No, it's late. I think you should hit the sack now."

"Please Daddy. I really want to go with you to walk her. I haven't seen her all day."

"Oh ok, let's tell Mommy that we're home and then get Sam to walk."

The house is dark and quiet when we walk in from the garage door. All the lights are off and not a sound could be heard. Not even the sound from Samantha as she usually is the first to run down the stairs after hearing the alarm chimes go off when the door opens.

Thinking something is wrong, I tell Ciana to wait back in the car and then I get my gun from the desk draw in my den and load it with bullets.

I slowly creep up the stairs with my gun in my right-hand calling Saundra's name.

Not a sound.

When I reach the floor where the bedrooms are there is still not a sound as I continue to call Saundra's name softly. I then slowly open our bedroom door and notice that there is a flickering light coming from under the bathroom door.

I walk up to the bathroom door softly and quietly, and then I fling it open fast and hard pointing the gun as Saundra jumps up out of her bath water yanking her earphones off her head and Samantha jumping up startled as well.

"Ahhh!! Richard what are you doing!?!" Saundra asks.

"Shit, Saundra, you scared the shit out of me!" I tell her.

"I scared you?! You scared me!" Saundra says.

"I'm sorry hun. When I didn't hear from you all day and seeing all the lights off made me a bit paranoid."

"I had my earphones on listening to music and I must have fallen asleep while soaking in the tub. Samantha was asleep on the floor as well. I'm sorry if I got you worried."

"It's okay. I'm sorry for almost shooting you." I say with a chuckle. "Let me go and get Ciana. I told her to wait in the car until the coast is clear."

"Ok, I'll get dressed and come downstairs." replied Saundra.

I go to the garage and open the door for Ciana.

"Hey, come on in. Your mother was just upstairs in the bathroom and didn't hear us."

"Heyyy Ciana, how was your day?" asked Saundra.

"Hi mommy! It was greeaatt!" yelled Ciana.

"That's sooo wonderful!" Saundra replied.

"Guess what we did?" Ciana says without giving her mother a chance to guess. "We went through an underground tunnel where there were huge limestone hanging down from the ceiling and it was like a whole different world which was dark and gloomy. I think my eyes were tricked from being in the cavern for so long because when we got out it was very hard to see clearly.

After that we got lost in this maze made out of tall bushes, and then after that we went to the toy museum where there was lots of interesting candies and toys. We actually saw a coconut candy bar that was the color of red, white, and blue. Some of the toys weren't really toys though but were mainly souvenirs. And then after that we went to the car museum where we saw lots of different cars from back in the day. It was really fun and exciting!"

"Well I know that you are excited and want to tell me all about it but it's way past your bedtime. You can tell me all about it tomorrow. Get ready for bed now." states Saundra.

"I was going to go with Daddy to walk Samantha."

"I think that you should just let your father go and take her and you just get ready for bed."

"Honey, it's cool. I'm just going to walk her quickly, so she can just go to bed when we get back. She's still a bit excited about the day. We won't take long." I say.

"It's ten forty-five; she really needs to go to bed."

"Come on, Love. She'll be okay. We'll be right back."

"Alright, well hurry back. I really want her to get to bed soon."

"We'll be back sooner than you can blink an eye. Let's go, Ciana." I tell her.

The night was clear and brisk but dry for late March. The night seemed brighter than usual due to the full moon that encompassed the clear night sky and had seemed unusually quiet since there weren't many people out or cars on the road.

"Where are we walking her to?" asked Ciana.

"We'll just go to that park area two blocks up. She seems to go to the bathroom quicker there and I'm definitely not trying to walk all around the mulberry bush just to get her to take a crap."

"Ok. I'll hold the leash." she says.

"It's okay sweetheart. I'll hold the leash since she's pulling. I guess she may have to use the bathroom after all. We better walk faster."

No sooner than I said that, Samantha saw a cat run across the road and broke free from my grip to chase it.

"Samantha!" Ciana yells and then runs after Samantha to try and catch her.

Ciana dashes across the street to try and catch Samantha, just when a blue sedan comes flying down the road at 50 miles per hour, slams on its breaks and hits Ciana as she's crossing the road. The impact flips her into the air landing her fifteen feet further down the street from the point of impact. The blue sedan stops and then speeds right off into the dark night.

I stare in shock and with an empty sinking feeling in the pit of my stomach I run to Ciana who is lying motionless in the middle of the road. Her brown bouncy curly hair now dark, wet, and heavily laden with blood.

"CIANA!! OH MY GOD! PLEASE GOD, PLEASE GOD LET HER BE OKAY!

I fall on my knees reaching out to hold Ciana, cradling her in my arms while blood seeps out of her nose and mouth, afraid to let her go out of my arms.

"Ciana, please wake up. Please answer me, Ciana, please. SOMEONE HELP ME PLEASE! SOMEONE PLEASE CALL AN AMBULANCE!" I scream as tears start to flow down my face. "Ciana, please wake up!"

An ambulance can be heard in the distant background as people come running to me trying to offer their help.

As the ambulance pulls up, I'm is still holding Ciana in my arms. My shirt is now stained with her blood as her breathing seem to become fainter and fainter. The paramedics place her lifeless body on the stretcher while administering oxygen in an attempt to stabilize her.

A passerby who knows us grabs a hold of Samantha and offers to take her back to the house while I ride in the ambulance with Ciana.

As the ambulance speeds off racing its way to the hospital the paramedics continue to try and stabilize her. I pick up my cell phone in order to call Saundra and inform her of what's happening.

"Saundra, something bad happened." I say to her.

"What's going on?! Where are the both of you? What is that noise in the background?" she asked.

"We're in an ambulance. Something terrible just happened. Ciana was hit by a car."

"Oh my God!" yelled Saundra. "What hospital are you going to?"

"We are headed to Maryland Medical."

"I'm headed out there right now."

"Wait a few minutes. Someone is dropping Samantha over there in a few."

"Alright. I'll be there as soon as possible."

"Ok, see you then."

The paramedics work diligently to continue to try and stabilize Ciana as her breathing becomes more and more faint. As they reach the hospital, the paramedics rapidly move towards the building and take her into the shock trauma unit to try and save her life.

I stand outside the unit pacing back and forth as Saundra finally reaches the waiting area and sees me. She immediately runs towards me and embraces me while tears flow down her cheeks.

"She's going to be okay." I tell her in a soothing assured voice as I keep my embrace tight.

It seemed like an eternity but when I looked at the clock on the wall it was actually only 40 minutes that had elapsed, when an older grey-haired doctor wearing surgical scrubs comes out of the unit walking towards me and Saundra. As he gets closer, he takes off his eyeglasses and wipes the sweat off his forehead with the handkerchief that he pulled out from his pants' pocket.

"Good evening, Mr. and Mrs. Clayton. I am Doctor Stevenson." said the doctor.

"How is she?!" exclaimed Saundra.

Putting down his head and looking towards the floor, "....I'm sorry. We did all that we could do. Unfortunately, we could not save her."

My heart seemed to sink deep down into my stomach, while my legs seemed to turn into jelly and couldn't hold up my body any longer. I fell to my knees as a nauseating feeling came resonating throughout my entire body.

"Oh God, no! Please God, NO! This can't be happening." I say while on my knees in a ball crying to God.

Saundra tries to pick me back up unto my feet unsuccessfully as I feel overwhelmed with pain and such a hurt feeling as if the walls had just caved in on me. When I'm finally able to climb to my feet, I try very hard to compose myself so that I could gather up enough strength to see her.

"Doctor, can we see her?" I ask trying to hold my composure.

"Yes, you both can. The room is cleared out for your privacy."

"Saundra and I walk slowly but steadily towards the room, hesitating for a moment before opening the door. When walk in, it is eerily quiet in the room. All the machines are turned off and Ciana is lying motionless in the bed. Her body no longer warm and malleable but now cold and rigid. The glow of light which always seemed to encompass her body is now dark.

"I'm so sorry, Ciana. I should have held onto Samantha tighter. Please forgive me." I say softly in her ear.

Saundra sits in the chair next to the bed crying and barely able to look at Ciana lying in the bed. Her sorrow then turns to anger as she looks at me next to her.

"How could you let this happen." She says in a harsh tone. "Why weren't you holding her hand? I even told you not to take her out because it was too late, but you did not want to listen to me. You just had to do what you wanted to do. If you had just listened to me, we wouldn't be here, and she would have been in her bed sleeping right now."

I didn't say a word, not knowing what to say and realizing that she could be right. I just stared at Ciana thinking that her eyes will open up at any moment and hoping to see that infamous smile plastered on her face, but of course, it didn't happen.

By the time Saundra and I left the hospital it was about 2:30 in the morning. We reached the house by 3:00 am and were knocked out in bed by 3:15am, having gone through the motions in a surreal dreamlike state, thinking that maybe this is just a nightmare that we would both wake up from.

Chapter 13

It is 8:00 a.m. on Sunday morning when I am awakened by the whining of Samantha outside our bedroom door desiring to go outside to use the 'bathroom.' Saundra is still in bed completely emerged with the blanket over her head.

I get up and put on my sweats and my old beat-up dog-walking sneakers on my feet and then walk towards the door to open it up as I see Samantha sitting in front of it just waiting for me to take her out. I walk towards Ciana's room and open the door. Her bed is completely made up as it was the day before. It had just hit me that she is not here, and she will no longer be here. The realization just hit me that it was not a dream. It was real. She's dead. Killed by a hit and run driver.

As I walk Samantha, I take the same path as I did the night before and stand at the spot where Ciana took off chasing after Samantha right before crossing the street that the car had hit her on. I stood there for about ten minutes in a zone just looking up and down the street envisioning the car speeding down the street.

"Why didn't I just hold onto the leash tighter?" I say to myself. "Why the hell didn't I just leave her in the house and just walked the dog by myself? She would still be alive today."

When I return home from walking Samantha, Saundra is still in bed with the covers still over her head.

"Sweetheart, please try to get up." I say as I pull back the blanket and whisper into her ear.

"I don't want to. Please just let me be." Saundra says clearly annoyed then covering back her head with the blanket without saying another word.

I then hear the doorbell ring and go downstairs to answer the door. Samantha races to the door before I could get there and started to bark wildly. When I open up the door, two uniformed Baltimore City Police officers and a plain clothed man is standing in front of me at the door.

"Hello Mr. Clayton, I am detective Roberts, and this is officer Branson and officer Hailey. Can we come in and speak with you for a moment?"

"Sure, come in." I say softly as I open the door wider inviting them in.

"We wanted to let you know that we found the car that hit your daughter and apprehended the driver of that car at around 4:00 am this morning." Detective Roberts stated.

"That's good. I'm very glad that you were able to get the culprit so quickly. If you don't mind though, I really need to get some rest since my wife and I didn't sleep much last night."

"Well, before we go, Sir, there's something that we need to tell you that is very important, because this information will probably hit the news."

"What is it?"

"The man who was driving the car that hit your daughter was a person who you had previously represented in court."

"What!?! Who?" I ask as I think about all of my previous clients and if there were any cases that I lost thinking that someone might have retaliated. Did Darion Tibbs retaliate because I didn't take his case?

"Rodney Whinebeck."

"What?!?" My heart sunk deep into my stomach and my face became flushed, shocked at the information that I had just received. "Are you serious!! Why? Was this intentional?"

"We are pretty sure that this was just a random act, very extemporaneous. He apparently was celebrating getting out of jail and getting off of that murder charge, then he got intoxicated and stole a vehicle to joy ride in." said Detective Roberts. "I just wanted to inform you of this information before you heard it on the news first."

"Thank you for telling me this." I said in a low somber voice.

"We have charged him with vehicular manslaughter, grand theft auto, and firearm possession."

"Firearm possession?? You found a gun on him?"

"Yes, we found a fully loaded .45."

"Fuck!" I said softly closing my eyes angry at myself thinking of the .45 caliber gun that killed Jerry Smith. 'Could this be the same weapon? The actual murder weapon!?' I thought to myself.

"Officers, thank you for coming by." I tell them as I open the door for them to leave.

As the officers leave, I sit down on the plush chair in the living room in a surreal moment thinking that this couldn't possibly be reality. The queasiness in my stomach worsened.

'If I had lost that case, Rodney would have still been in jail last night. He would be on his way to the state penitentiary and Ciana would still be alive today. Did I put my career and my ambitions before my own family?' I thought to myself as I sit here contemplating my actions.

Saundra comes down the stairs looking frazzled and disheveled in her robe and slippers. The once highly put together, intimidating corporate lawyer now looks like a homeless person who has given up on life.

"Who was at the door?" She asks in a soft voice as if she really didn't care.

"It was just a couple of neighbors who heard about the incident and wanted to come by to see if we needed any help with anything." I tell her clearly afraid to tell her the truth.

"Oh, alright." She states.

"First thing tomorrow we must go and make the necessary arraignments. I am really going to need you to be strong for me. This is going to be tough, but I am really going to need you. OK?"

"Yeah, sure." Saundra answers in a non-attentive way and then heads back upstairs to return to the bedroom.

I then pull out my phone and scroll down the address book looking over all the people that I must call in order to inform them of the tragic news, however my mind keeps drifting back over to Rodney thinking that he is probably playing cards or watching T.V. at the jail right now without a care in the world, oblivious to his actions.

Chapter 14

It looks as though there are at least 300 people inside the First Baptist Church of Baltimore, where we are holding Ciana's funeral service. I have no idea who most of the people here are. I do, however, recognize a few faces though, besides our friends and family who have taken up the first four rows of the church pews. Some of the other people are clients that I had represented, attorneys who either knew me or heard of me, judges, and a few police officers that I had gone up against with in court. However, I do believe though that a lot of the people here are only here because they heard about this tragedy on the news and either they wanted to sympathize with the situation or exploit the situation.

One of the people who I believe are exploiting the situation is Councilman Raymond Watts. I've never met him personally however I do know that he is an opportunist who tries to show his face at every funeral in the city where the death was caused by some sort of violence, and then he sets up a podium outside of the churches or funeral homes and uses his bullhorn to speak to the incoming patrons about the city's crime and violence problem. He is constantly on T.V. voicing his opinion about something or another. It is no question that his motive is to try to run for Mayor in the next election cycle.

"Richard Clayton!" Councilman Watts yells to me to get my attention.

I turn around to him as he comes to approach me.

"Hello Mr. Clayton, I am Councilman Raymond Watts. I want to give you my sincere condolences for the loss of your daughter. I am really very sorry that you and your wife have to go through such a tragedy. I am doing my best to try to fight the crime in this city and want you to know that your daughter will always be remembered by me."

"Thank you for your condolences, councilman." I say as I start to turn away to head to the open casket holding Ciana, so I could see her one last time.

"Uh, Richard, before you go, I want you to know that if you need anything I am here to help. If you would like me to speak to this crowd today, I have no problem doing so. I think that I can offer everyone a comforting word."

"Thank you, councilman, but I think that we are good. I appreciate you offering though." I say trying not to be annoyed at his audacity asking me that as I'm about to view my daughter for the very last time.

I walk to the opened casket and look in. My knees almost buckle, and I felt a knot in my chest as if I was about to throw up. She looked so beautiful and peaceful. I just wanted to hold her for one last time, but I knew that I couldn't. I have never felt such pain before in my life. The pain of loss was so unbearable that I crumpled and fell to the floor crying in disbelief. Councilman Watts comes up to me again and rests his hand on the back of my shoulder and uses his other arm to help get me up. I then hold in my composure and return to my seat in the first pew sitting next to Saundra.

The choir had gotten on stage and started to sing Michael Jackson's song, "Gone Too Soon," and then sing "Fly" by Celine Dion, before the pastor started his sermon.

"Good morning ladies and gentlemen." Pastor James says as he starts his sermon. "We are gathered here to celebrate the life and homegoing of Ciana Lynn Clayton. Although her life was short lived, we must still acknowledge the glory and happiness that she had bestowed upon others. We must not morn but be joyous that she is now in the arms of our Almighty Father in Heaven. No one ever thinks that they'll be saying a final goodbye to a youngster; they seem too full of life and all the promise of things to come. Their futures stretch out before them – like a book waiting to be read – you don't expect to find yourself in a place like this, on a day like today, to mark the end of a life that had hardly even started. But here we all are, saying farewell to this beautiful little child, Ciana, long before her time – and that just doesn't feel at all right. Although Ciana was only with us for such a very short period of time, she had a huge personality and it was hard not to notice her. That's one of the things that make her sudden loss so very difficult to come to terms with – you always felt that she was going to be a fun child to watch growing up. Knowing that isn't going to happen is very hard to accept. I'm sure many of us here have our own special memories of her. At a time like this, there are so many different feelings – despair, anger, sorrow, confusion – and so many questions. Why did it happen? Why Ciana? Amid all that, our hearts go out to her parents, Richard and Saundra Clayton for the great burden that they bear today and will continue to bear in the coming days. Today, it's difficult to even begin to talk of "comfort"– but in the months and years ahead, as we remember little Ciana I hope we'll all gain strength from realizing, as we look back on her life, just how much of an affect she had on us in the short time we knew her and what a super little girl Ciana was. I would now like to bring up Ciana's father, Richard Clayton to say a few words."

I get up and approach the podium on the stage feeling all the eyeballs watching my every move as I walk. I try to concentrate on the words of what I will be saying and not the emotion behind the words.

"Good morning... Ciana was everything to me. When I saw my wife give birth to her, she was encompassed in light. I knew right then that her name would be Ciana, which means light. She was a beam of light. She was the strand of light that gave me motivation when I needed it, laughter when I needed it, and joy when I needed it. I love her and will miss her tremendously. Thank you."

The crowd was very quiet when I finished my speech and as I went to go sit back down next to Saundra. The choir then sang another song. Unfortunately, my mind was no longer here, so I have no idea what that song was or what anyone else had said about Ciana afterwards. I just knew that I wanted this day to finally end. After the funeral services, Saundra and I start to leave out with our family members in order to attend the burial. We chose not to have a public burial because we wanted our last goodbyes to be private and personal without all the hoopla of people around us that we didn't know.

"Mr. Clayton!" I hear a male's voice call out to me. I turn around, to recognize who it is.

"Jeremiah? Hey, how are you? You came!" I state saying to Jeremiah Scott.

"I am really sorry for what has happened." He says.

"Thank you, Jeremiah. How have you been?" I ask.

"I have been doing good. I went back to school and got my GED. I always appreciated how you spoke to me that last time. You inspired me to want to look into law."

"You're welcome. I guess I saw your potential. I'm sorry but I do have to go, but feel free to contact me when everything settles."

"Ok, thanks Mr. Clayton."

When Saundra and I get to the burial ground, we say a prayer and our goodbyes once again.

"Goodbye, my beautiful light. Your light will always shine in my heart. I'm always going to miss you. Goodbye Ciana."

Chapter 15

It's been three weeks since the death of Ciana. I'm still reeling from the emotion caused by the funeral held a week ago; however, I realize that I must now try to move on and go back to the office. However, after having been away from my office for three weeks made me really contemplate my life choices and my career.

'I'm a criminal defense attorney. I help criminals get off. Why am I doing this? It's not like I make a lot of money. I'm a Public Defender for God's sake. Why the hell am I doing this for?' These thoughts keep infiltrating my mind as I'm driving in my car heading to the office.

As I get in my building and head for my office, I notice that it is unusually quiet although everyone is in the office today. People seem to look up at me with a sorrowful look and then avert their eyes back down at their desks as I head toward my office door. At my door there are literally at least fifty condolence cards taped on the door and several baskets of flowers at the foot of it. I leave everything the way it is as I walk through the door into my office and close the door behind me. On my desk is still the thick Rodney Whinebeck file left as it was when I left the office celebrating my big win three weeks ago.

I sit at my desk just staring at the folder neither opening it nor putting it away. 'This is the man who had killed my daughter.' I say to myself. 'I worked so hard for this man's freedom just so he could take away my daughter's life. She would be still alive today had I lost.'

Just as I was in a trance-like state, someone knocks on my door which snaps me out of my deep thoughts.

"Come in." I say.

"Hey Richard, welcome back. I know that this time can be very hard for you so if you need to take any more time off, I will understand and grant you as much time as you need." Fletcher says to me in a consoling voice.

"Thanks Fletcher, but I better keep my mind busy with work or I'll go crazy."

"Okay, but just know that if you do need more time it is there for you. You are one of our best attorneys, so I will accommodate to your needs." he stated.

"Thanks Fletcher. I'll keep that in mind." I tell him.

"I do, however, need you to go to the grief counselor psychiatrist this afternoon though. It is protocol for all state employees who had gone through some type of tragedy."

"I really am okay. I really don't think that is really necessary."

"Richard, I'm not suggesting it; I am telling you that you must go. If anything goes wrong by you not going, we would be liable. I had Monica set up an appointment for 2:30 this afternoon with Dr. Frount at the health department on Charles Street."

"Alright, I'll be there." I state softly and unwillingly.

As the day went on, I could barely concentrate on any of my new cases. The question that kept on burdening my mind and thought process was, 'Why am I really doing this?'

All that I could focus on was the life and the sudden death of Ciana. All I could think of was that my "Light" was gone and it was all my fault. I now feel that I dwell in the darkness I created.

When 2:00 finally came around, I realize that I had barely done any work today. I gather my belongings and head out to go to the city health department building four blocks away. Instead of driving I decide to walk even though it is raining outside and a bit cold and breezy from the early April weather.

I walk in a trance-like state not caring about the drizzling rain hitting my wide-brim hat as my shoulders start to get soaked and my socks feeling a bit damp from stepping into a few puddles.

When I reach the doctor's office I knock on the door and a short, frumpy bald white guy opens the door and sticks out his hand for a handshake.

"Hello, I'm Dr. Frount. Please come in." the man beckons.

"Hi, I'm Richard Clayton. I have a 2:30 appointment." I say as I shake the man's hand.

"Ahh, yes. Please sit down."

The office was small but cozy. It just had one plush recliner chair, one loveseat, and a small table with a writing pad and a folder on it. This was definitely not what I expected. I then just decide to seat on the loveseat.

"I see here that you recently had a serious tragedy just happen to you. Was it the death of your daughter?" Dr. Frount asks.

I hesitate for a moment thinking about the stupidity of the question just asked. 'Of course it was the death of my daughter, what else would it be you moron.' I thought to myself but reframed from answering him in that way.

"Yes, that is correct." I tell him.

"Are you in any type of grief counseling?" Dr. Frount asks.

"No."

"Do you know what stage of the grieving process that you may be in?"

"What stage of the grieving process that I may be in?? I don't even know what that means." I tell him.

"Well, there are usually five stages of grief. The first one is shock or denial. This is where you can't believe that your loved one is really gone. This stage could actually last for several weeks. The second stage is pain or guilt. Here is where you think of everything you wish you would have or wouldn't have done which could have prevented the loved one's death. You may feel incredible guilt and unbelievable pain. The third stage is usually anger or bargaining. During this stage you think, 'Why me?' or 'Why them?' questions. You could get very mad or angry and start blaming others. Or you could bargain and say, 'I will do anything to have them back again.' Then the fourth stage is depression. You could isolate yourself from external or even internal behaviors and activities. You would want to get on with your life, but you feel depressed because your loved one isn't around anymore. And then the last stage is acceptance and hope. You might not be actually happy with the loss, but you have come to terms with things and look forward to your own future. You may experience one or all of the stages and it may present itself in various orders. Do you now understand and know what stage that you might be in?"

"Yes, I understand. I guess I might be in the guilt stage. Had I not gotten my client off she would still be alive today."

"Well, you really can't blame yourself in these matters."

"What are you talking about? It's a fact! Had I not gotten my client off he would have remained in jail and she would still be alive today!"

I sit here hearing but not really listening to Dr. Frount's montage of how life comes with surprises and God's plan, and how we must move on because life goes on, but it registered in my mind with no avail. I knew that it was Rodney who killed my daughter and it was me that got him out of jail a day prior to the incident.

"Mr. Clayton, I am going to recommend a grief counseling group for you to attend. In this group you would be around other parents who had lost their children and how they dealt with it. There are really good techniques on how to live after a death. I think you should attend and if you are married, your wife should attend as well. Many marriages don't succeed after such a tragedy. Here is a list of local group sessions that you could attend. I really highly recommend this."

"I'll consider it."

I gather my belongings and headed back to the office. The rain has stopped however it is still very wet outside, so I continue to get my pants legs wet by the splashing pools of water on the ground. I take out the list of support groups that Dr. Frount had given to me and crumple it up and toss it in the garbage can at the corner of the street.

'He didn't know what he was talking about. I'm definitely not going to take advice from someone who doesn't know what's it's like to lose a child.' I think to myself as I race back to the office trying not to get upset for feeling as though I wasted my time. So, I guess this is what Jerry Smith's mother was talking about.

Chapter 16

When I got home, I see Saundra curled up on the couch watching the local news.

"Hey honey, how are you doing today?" I ask.

Saundra doesn't answer me and continues to watch the television.

"Hey honey, are you okay?" I ask her again.

Once again, she doesn't answer and continues to watch the television.

After about 10 minutes of silence, Saundra finally opens her mouth to speak.

"The man who killed our daughter was the same man that you defended in court. Did you know that?"

"Ahh, yes I did." I hesitated as I cleared my throat.

"When did you find this out?" she asks.

"The day after the accident."

"So why didn't you tell me then?"

"I just didn't want you to get more devastated by the incident."

"Richard, I told you time in and time again to stop being a public defender. I even offered you a position at my firm, but you chose not to even consider it. Had you just decided to quit, Ciana would be still alive today. I blame you for her death." Saundra says very calmly.

"I am not the one to blame here." I tell her, knowing that I have already been blaming myself for what had happened.

"You defended him and got him off. Who else is there to blame?"

I knew that she was right, I just didn't want to admit that to her. I see that she is in the 'anger stage' that Dr. Frount was mentioning.

"I went to a psychiatrist today and he mentioned something about attending group grief counseling. Maybe we should consider going."

"Is this going to bring back Ciana?" She says sarcastically.

"Of course not."

"Then why, Richard, would I waste my time and go to something like that?"

"Because maybe it could help us get over this grief and strengthen our marriage."

"I'm not interested. It's you who I blame, and I will never forgive you for that." Saundra says as she goes upstairs into our bedroom and closes the door behind her.

"I understand." I say softly to myself as I slump down on the couch with my head draped over the pillows on the arm of couch.

"I really can't believe that this is happening. It's like a nightmare that I can't seem to wake up from.

Chapter 17

I woke up this morning with a serious neck cramp from sleeping on the sofa in the living room all night, still fully dressed wearing the same clothes that I had on yesterday. Saundra never came back out of the bedroom since our last discussion yesterday, so I had just figured that it would probably behoove me not to sleep in our bedroom last night. Although I would have just left to go back to the office this morning without acknowledging her, I did need to take a shower and then change clothes into another suit which of course, is in our bedroom closet.

I go upstairs and knock on the bedroom door. "Saundra, can you unlock the door please. I need to get ready for work." I ask her as I wait to get in.

Saundra opens the door without saying a word, still dressed in her pajamas and then she just crawls back into the bed. I say nothing and just go into the bathroom to take a shower and get ready for work. As I get fully dressed and about to leave the room, I make one more attempt to reach out to her.

"Hey Honey, I'm going to walk Sam and then I'm leaving out for work. Do you think that we can sit down and talk later today when I get home? I really think that we need to talk about everything, so we can both heal and move forward."

Saundra releases a heavy sigh, and then moans however say nothing.

When I get into my office, my head is spinning, and I find it very hard to concentrate on my work. I have court today at the District courthouse on North Avenue with presiding Judge Ransin.

I have three cases with him today however have no idea what they are because I have yet to read the case files. Even after sitting here at my desk for the past 20 minutes, knowing that court starts in about an hour at 9:30am, I have no motivation to open up the files.

I play the two songs on my iPod that I usually play every time before going to court in order to try to boost my motivation and morale; Bill Conti's Gonna Fly Now and LL's Momma Said Knock You Out, as I get up from my desk and start to shadow box in my office to try to raise my spirit.

I do get enough strength to read the cases however my mind keeps drifting back to Saundra and her wellbeing. I pick up my cell phone and try to call her to see if she is okay. The phone rings several times and then just goes to voice mail so I decided to leave a message. "Hey Honey, I am just checking in on you. I hope that you are feeling better." After, I hung up I thought about the message that I just left. Hoping that she is feeling better? That was stupid to say. She is not sick she is depressed and hurt because of the death of our daughter. What was I thinking?

I pack up my folders and put on my jacket to head to my car so that I could go to the courthouse. When I reach the courthouse and park, I stay sitting in the car for a few minutes trying to get my composure and my mind back on my work. I take a couple deep breaths with my eyes closed and then I open them with a focused determined look on my face and then step out of the car, making sure that my life is so compartmentalized that my only focus is on the defendants.

I walk into the courtroom still holding onto the same beam of focus that I had coerced myself to have moments earlier. Luckily the first case to be called was one of mine.

Although this case itself is a very difficult one since it deals with heroin possession, all I had to do today was move it to the Circuit court which automatically postpones it for a different day that is available on the docket. My second case wasn't so easy though. Not only did it take two hours to be called, it is a case of a young lady in her early 20s who had her driver's license suspended and yet she had still continued to drive her car which unfortunately caused an accident by hitting another vehicle while she was paying more attention to her incoming text message than the other drivers on the road. On any other day I would have handled this case with ease. I would have persuaded the judge to just give her probation before judgment, however could I really do that today in good conscience? My child was just hit and killed by a reckless driver! Not to mention that that driver was the same person that I helped get off in the first place. What if I got this young woman off and she did the same thing again? This time she might kill someone's child or parent or spouse.

When the case was called a very young chic-looking African American lady approaches the defense table and stood right next to me. I couldn't help but think about Ciana. Ciana would never be this woman's age. This woman's recklessness could have seriously injured or killed someone. Here I am standing here thinking more about my dead daughter than defending this woman in court. I am actually feeling as though I am getting more and more upset over this woman's careless actions. Can I really be non-biased here?

"Good morning." Judge Ransin says.

"Good morning, your Honor." I say as I nudge my client to greet him as well.

"Counsel, your client is charged with a number of serious traffic citations here, however the state is willing to drop all of them except for the Driving while Suspended charge in which they are recommending a one-year probation. Is she willing to take a plea for that or does she wish to go to trial?"

I look at my client and ask her what her wishes are as I put my own conflicts aside. She then hesitates for a moment and then nods her head in order to agree to the plea deal.

"Yes, your Honor, my client will accept the plea."

"Fair enough." He says and then looks at my client. "Ms. Cassidy, how old are you?"

"I am 22." She states.

"How far did you get in school?"

"I am a junior at Maryland."

"Do you understand that by accepting a guilty plea, I have the right to either accept the prosecution's recommendation or deny it and sentence you to what I feel would be appropriate?"

"Yes, I understand."

"By pleading guilty you are acknowledging that the alleged conduct is made punishable by law and that you could face a year in jail, or a $1,000 fine, or both."

"Yes, I understand."

"By pleading guilty you are also admitting to the charges made against you."

"Yes."

"Do you know and understand the rights that you are waiving by pleading guilty, including the right to a jury trial, the right not to incriminate yourself, and the right to confront and cross-examine your accusers."

"Yes, I do understand."

"Also know that if you are not a U.S. citizen, you risk deportation."

"Yes, I understand. I am American."

"Did anyone force you into accepting this plea?"

"No."

"Are you pleading guilty because you in fact did drive your vehicle with a suspended license which caused an accident?"

"Yes, that is correct."

"Ms. Cassidy, I will accept your plea and I will accept the State's recommendation of a one-year probation period. You will also pay $200 in fines and court costs."

"Thank you, sir." Ms. Cassidy and I seemed to say in unison.

I then sit back down in the pews waiting for my last case to be called. I haven't seen nor heard from the defendant yet so more than likely he would get an FTA if he doesn't show up by the time they call the case.

Almost immediately my last case was called next, so I stood back up and walked back to the defense table.

The clerk shouts out the name of my client again however no one answered.

"Counsel, have you heard from your client today?" Judge Ransin asks me.

"No, your Honor. I have not seen nor heard from him." I replied.

"Ok. I will mark this as a Failure to Appear and issue a bench warrant." The judge stated.

"Ok your Honor. I will inform him if he contacts me. Thank you."

I was very glad that my caseload was done for the day, so I decided that I would just leave here and go straight home instead of returning to the office since it was already nearly 4:00.

When I get into my car, I decide to call Saundra to let her know that I will be coming home early and maybe we can have a good sit-down talk.

I turn back on my cell phone and push the favorite's button with the one attached to her name on it to quickly dial her number. Once again, the phone keeps ringing and then goes directly into voicemail. Ok, now I'm frustrated. Her passive aggressive attitude is driving me crazy. I just hang up without leaving a message and head towards home.

When I reach the house and pull into the garage, I notice that Saundra's car is not here. I really wish that she had just let me know that she was not going to be home. When I get into the house, Samantha is waiting at the door to go out for her walk. I put my stuff down and get her leash and attach it to her collar. I hurry her up as we walk to the dog park so that I can get back in the house to wait for Saundra to come back home.

Luckily Samantha uses the bathroom pretty quickly, so we head back to the house within 15 minutes of us leaving. When I get back in the house, it seems eerily odd for some reason. I have this 'off' feeling that something is not quite right but I just can't put my finger on it. I brush off that weird feeling and sit on the couch and turn on the television to CNN.

After about an hour I find myself starting to dose off on the couch in my suit. I already slept in my clothes on the couch last night; I'm surely not going to do that again tonight. So I go upstairs to change my clothes into something more comfortable, preferably some comfortable sweat clothes.

When I get to the bedroom I just stand at the threshold of the door looking around the room. For some reason it looks very odd, but I still just can't put my finger on it. Everything is very neat and clean but looks sort of empty. I then walk into the closet and realized that my biggest fear has come into fruition. All of Saundra's clothes are gone. This can't be. I look into her draws and again, there is nothing in them. Everything of hers is gone; her clothes, shoes, purses, jewelry, hair products, books, everything, GONE!

I look in the bathroom and notice that there is a letter posted to the bathroom mirror. I reach for it and pull it down to read.

[Dear Richard, I'm sorry that things came to this. I know that you love me and want to help us get through this time of tragedy but are unsure of what to do or what to say as you watch me drifting further and further away from you and the everyday life we use to lead together. I find it hard to articulate what is actually going on inside my mind. One moment I feel as though we can work through this and rebuild the life we once had, however, on a different moment, I feel as though I hate you and fully blame you for the death of our daughter. At times I feel totally empty, as if every particle of my being has been sucked into a black hole. At other times I feel crushed, my spirit devoid of human warmth, and these are feelings I simply cannot control. When I ask myself if I still love you, I seem unsure how to answer. It's not that I don't love you, because I know that somewhere inside this depressed person I've become, I do love you very much, but depression has robbed me of the ability to show it right now. You may question whether my love is real anymore because I blame you for Ciana's death, but please know that it's not that I no longer love you, it's just that I'm finding it hard to connect to that part in me which connects to you. The truth is, I can't connect to you because I can't find a way to connect to myself right now. This all may seem difficult to understand and I think this is what makes being depressed so hard to deal with. Nothing in my behavior or thinking makes sense to me. I know that makes me hard to understand and sometimes hard to be around. I am seeking the help that I need right now and am doing what I can to find a way forward through this difficult time. The only thing that I do know is that at this moment, I cannot be under the same roof with you. I cannot be with you. I will always love you and wish you the best. – Saundra.]

I then pick up my cell phone and frantically dial her phone. Again, her phone rings and then goes to voicemail. This time I leave a message.

"Saundra, you left me?! Why didn't you just talk to me? Please call me back and talk to me. At least call me and tell me where you are."

As the hours continued to drag by, I had probably called her at least 10 times to no prevail. As I lay in the bed I keep the phone laying right next to me by my side and tried to get some sleep, hoping that she would eventually get the desire to call me in the middle of the night.

As I lay here in my bed, the dead silence of the house is disturbing. My mind reminisces back to the happy times we all had spent in this house. It wasn't even more than a month ago when the house was full of joy, happiness, and laughter, now it is just dark and heavy with despair and sadness.

When I wake up the next morning my body feels as though I have not slept in weeks. I feel very lethargic and unmotivated to do anything but sleep hoping that I could wake up from this crazy bad dream.

Saundra and I use to speak to each other every single day for the past 15 years, now I have no idea at all where she is at. I call her once more to see if she would answer.

"Hello." Saundra answers.

"Saundra?! Where are you? What's going on?" I ask.

She hesitates for a moment. "Did you read my letter? I must leave."

"What?! Why?! Look, we can get through this. Many couples have succeeded despite the loss of a child. We can do this as well. I love you, Saundra. Let's work through this." I say to her pleading my case.

"Richard, I can no longer do this. I am not happy with you anymore. I think that I have not been happy with us for a very long time even before the death of

Ciana. You have always put your defendants before your family and although I didn't agree with it, I supported it. Her death just put the nail in the coffin. I can no longer say; 'at least we have Ciana' in order to stay and try to make this marriage work." She says.

"Please don't do this. We can make this better, I promise you. I need you, Saundra, I love you, please don't leave."

"Goodbye Richard. I wish you the best." She says abruptly before I'm able to finish my sentence and then hangs up her phone.

I continue to sit on the bed staring in space still with the phone in my hand finding it very hard to believe how everything has just turned out over the past few weeks. I really can't believe that I lost my daughter and my wife in less than a month.

I feel empty. I feel sick, and distraught. I can't focus on anything. I can't even compartmentalize like I was able to before in order for me to even concentrate on any work. There is no way that I can go into work today. How would it even be remotely possible that I could concentrate on any of my cases if I went to work? I have to just call in sick and have Monica give my cases to someone else.

My legs down to my feet feel extremely heavy and sluggish as I head down the stairs to my den to open up a new bottle of Salignac Cognac. The alcohol seems to go smoothly down my throat as I drink straight from the bottle. A drink that I would normally sip with ease I now easily gulp the drink down my throat with no concerned of intoxication.

One gulp. Two gulps. Three gulps. Four. I count to myself as I gulp down the alcohol. I sit at my desk in the den trying to finish the entire 750 milliliter bottle of Cognac in one sitting. As my head starts to spin, I become very dizzy and try to force myself to stay alert as I pull out my gun from the desk draw along with a box of .45 colt bullets. I then load two bullets into the revolving chamber before placing the weapon on top of the desk.

The alcohol is now taking a very strong effect on me and I feel as though that I am going to pass out however I do my best to resist the urge. I pick up the gun with my left hand with my thumb on the trigger and the barrel pointing towards me as my hand still rest on the desk. The barrel is pointing towards my head between my eyes as I take another swig of cognac.

I stare at the barrel of the gun staring back at me as it rests in my hand on the desk with my thumb still resting on the trigger.

I take another few gulps and end up finishing the bottle and then stare intently at the gun's barrel that I have pointing at me. My mind floods with images on Saundra, Ciana, and Samantha. I see flashbacks of all our family vacations and all the great times that we all shared together. I see the discussions that I enjoyed with Ciana and see the light in her eyes. I see how Saundra and I met. I even see the day we got Samantha when she was a small puppy at the shelter. Tears start to flow out of my eyes as the memories and the guilt collides with each other.

My thumb is feeling the smoothness of the trigger as it starts to add pressure.

POW!

All I saw was a bright flash and now just darkness.

Chapter 18

The feel of the long blades of grass pressing against the left side of my face with the warm sun beaming down on the right side of my face, and the sound I hear of water trickling from a stream in the distance all made me open my eyes. I get up from lying on the grass and sit up to look around the beautiful meadow that I am now sitting in, and wondering where the hell I am.

I stand up to look around my surroundings. No buildings. No people. No nothing except a big vast field with grass greener than I have ever seen before and a sky bluer than the deepest blue I had ever come across and crystal-clear water running down a small brook.

What happened? Where am I? Am I dead? Am I dreaming? What did I do? So many questions that I just cannot figure out the answers to.

I walk over to the brook and place my hands in the cold running water. This water is as cold as ice, and so clear that I can see my fingers as clearly as I can see them out of the water. I then cup my hands together to capture some of the water and put it in my mouth and then over my face. The water seemed to reinvigorate my total body and my soul. If I'm dead, why do I feel everything? Then again, if I'm dreaming, why do I feel everything?

In the distance I notice a small little brown log cabin with about four steps that reaches up to the front door with two big log pillars that holds up the canopy over the porch. It is about half a mile from where I am standing so I start walking towards it. Although I don't see any movement over there in the distance, somehow, I feel compelled to go to it and explore. As I get a little closer to the log cabin, I notice that the door is wide open, and it looks like there is a dim light shining from the inside of it.

As I finally approach the cabin, I start to walk up the stairs leading to the opened front door.

"HELLOOO?!" I yell. "Is anyone in here?"

I slowly walk through the threshold of the door and look inside. The cabin was very small with only two small 8-inch squared windows which were adjacent to each other and were perpendicular to the door. The floor was made out of the same wood as the walls but was smoother and more polished. The only furniture in the place was one chair and a small round table. On the table was a vase with the most beautiful fresh cut flowers that I had ever seen.

I go to sit on the chair and rest my left arm on the table as I move the chair to face the door so that I could immediately see if anyone walks in. As I look around, I pay attention to every nook and cranny in the room. Every little detail I try to notice. Maybe I am dead, and this is some type of weird Hell. Why would I be in such a beautiful place yet there is absolutely no one around. Not one other living soul. Not even an insect. Am I going to have to live like this for an eternity? Am I being punished for something? For what? What did I do?

I put my hands to my head and try to think of what had transpired that brought me to this situation. I really can't remember much of what happened yesterday. I remember that Ciana was killed by a hit and run driver a few weeks ago, I remember the funeral we had for her, and I remember going back to work afterwards, and I also remember Saundra leaving me. I got drunk and then I..., Shit! I think I shot myself with my gun! I must be dead! And if I'm dead, this must be some form of Hell or possibly purgatory!

As this new realization came to light, I immediately drop to my knees and start crying profusely, and then curled up in a fetal position and cried even more. With tears drenched down my face, I get out of the fetal position, yet I stay on my knees and clasp my hands together and start to pray.

"God, if you can hear me, please know that I am really sorry for what I have done to myself. Please, please, please forgive me. Please help me and take me out of here and allow me to join you in heaven."

Just as I said those words a bright strand of light begins to appear in the corner of the room. It becomes brighter and brighter until it is as bright as the sun. Even though it is as bright as the sun I am still able to directly look at it without hurting my eyes. The intense presence of this light is so incredibly overwhelming that I don't move, I just continue to stare at it with a sense of fear and amazement.

"Richard, you must strengthen your heart and your soul and continue with the purpose that you were given."

A voice seemed to come from the bright beam of light however it wasn't a voice that I could actually hear, it was a voice in my head, a hard thought, that came directly into my mind which was heard as clear as day as if it were heard by my ears.

"Who are you?" I ask fearfully.

"I am who I am. I am the Alpha and the Omega, I am the Creator and the Sustainer,"

An increased sense of fear overcame me. It was sort of the same type of fear that one would get when getting disciplined by a parent for doing something wrong, however it was one hundred times more intense. I was so scared that I began shaking uncontrollably and then placed my head on the floor in shame.

When I look up to see if the light is still there, I see the light transform into the shape of a man right before my eyes. This man was neither black or white, nor brown or yellow, but a man with without a race that could have been identified on Earth. He had a very wise and humble look on his face, yet it also looked very caring and full of love. He extends his arm inviting me to take hold of his hand which seems to be encompassed with a glowing light. I reach my hand out and take hold of his hand. The instant I grab his hand there is an intense bliss feeling of love which permeates throughout my entire body until it penetrates through to my soul. This love was very pure and unconditional. A love that was 100 times stronger and more intense than anything I have ever felt before, probably no one alive has ever felt this type of intensity of love before.

He leads me out the door of the cabin without saying a word and takes me onto the grassy meadow still holding onto my hand as we walk.

"Where are we going?" I ask

"I need to show you some things." He said, this time hearing his voice through my ears.

We continue to walk until we get to a large lake. He then places his hand into the water and puts his wet hand over my eyes then rubs them for a few seconds. When I open my eyes, I see several images and scenes in the sky. It actually looked like a movie trailer however I notice that the "star" was me. I stare at these images in awe, seeing my previous actions and my interaction with others in the world. The images were going at lightning speed however I was able to see and understand everything as if it were going at a regular normal pace.

"Take a look at your actions in life. You have always tried to do well and help others. You must learn to release your guilt and regret so that when you go back, you can continue on the path I set out for you."

"I don't want to go back. I lost everything back there. There is nothing for me to go back to." I said. "I want to stay here with you. I want to be with my daughter."

"You have not completed your purpose yet therefore you must return. You were given a gift and must help others with this gift. You must help those who have had unjust done onto them."

I keep my head looking towards the ground and keep defying his words trying to justify staying in this blank world of nowhere. As I look up again, I notice a young girl in the meadow running towards me. As she gets closer my heart sinks realizing that it is Ciana. I burst into tears and fall onto my knees. She has the biggest and brightest smile on her face as she runs up to me and hugs me. I cry uncontrollably and hug her tight pressing her against my chest. I am holding onto her so tight that when I was releasing her, I accidently rip a piece of cloth from her clothing in my hand.

"Oh my God! Honey, I miss you so much! How are you?" I say looking in unbelief as I stare at her.

"I am good, Daddy." She said.

"I am so sorry for what I had done. It was all my fault. I should have been there for you, but I wasn't. I should have always protected you, but I didn't. I am so sorry for representing the man who killed you. I am really sorry for letting you down."

"It wasn't your fault at all. You had nothing to do with it. You must let that go, Daddy. You must forgive yourself. Everything happens the way it is supposed to happen."

"Sweetheart, I am going to stay right here with you. I am not leaving you again."

"Daddy, you must go back. I am okay here. I am very happy. You must go back and complete your purpose. Don't worry I will see you again when the time is right."

"My purpose was taking care of you. I can't go back. I don't want to leave you again."

"Daddy, I want you to remember that I had always and will always believe in you. I must leave now but I'll see you again. I love you always."

"I love you always as well." I said to her.

She then rips off the part of cloth that I accidentally tore and places the piece of cloth in my hand, then closes my hand and hugs me once more. Just then, the man holds out his hand towards her and they started walking down the field hand in hand leaving me behind. I watched them as long as I could before they disappeared into the horizon. I lay back down on the grass and I cried. I cried so hard that I fell asleep.

Chapter 19

The hard wood floor was hurting the left side of my body. It feels as though I have been laying on it for days. I opened my eyes and noticed that I was lying on the floor of my den after having seemingly been passed out from being so intoxicated from drinking the whole bottle of Cognac. I look around while still on the floor and see Samantha lying on the floor just staring at me. I also see my gun resting about two feet away from me under my desk. When I sit up, I see a bullet hole in the wall behind me and a shell casing on the floor.

I feel all over my body and look to see where the bullet might have hit me however there are no bullet wounds that I can find. I guess I apparently must have missed. How could I have missed though? I had the gun pointed right towards my head. I saw the barrel of the gun. Did I dream all what I dreamt? Wow, it seemed so real.

As I start to get myself off of the floor, I notice a small piece of cloth that I was lying on. Is this...? It can't be. This can't be the cloth that Ciana gave to me in my dream. I pick it up and look at it thoroughly. Holy shit! I really did see her. It was real! I close my eyes for a moment trying to hold in my composure, realizing that all this was a gift from God. I probably did shoot myself in the head and died but God allowed me to see Ciana and then brought me back and healed me. Sitting here made me realize the miraculous power of God which also made me realize that He wanted me back here to complete the purpose that He destined for me.

I go over to my bookshelf and pull out the Bible and open it up to the Book of Job. I chose this story to read because it tells the story of a man who loses everything – his wealth, his family, his health – and wrestles with the question, Why?

In the end, Job acknowledges the sovereignty of God in his life and receives back more than he had before his trials.

I wanted to know my 'Why.' I wanted to know the purpose that I have in which I need to complete. All I know now is that my purpose no longer includes being a Public Defender for Baltimore City anymore.

Chapter 20

When I got to work the following day, I walk straight to Fletcher's office. He is on the phone speaking to someone, so I just stand by his door until he acknowledges me. He waves his hand to me as if to let me know to come on in, so I walk in and sit in one of the chairs in front of his desk and wait as he wraps up his conversation on the phone.

"What can I do for you Richard?" he says.

"Fletcher, I am turning in my resignation." I say as I hand him my resignation letter.

"I do understand what you might have been going through these past few weeks, but maybe it's just more time off that you need. I know that you are under a lot of stress and pressure. Do you think just taking a little more time off and come back in a few weeks would be conducive for you?"

"No, I think that it is best for me to leave the PD office for good. I can no longer in good conscience represent criminals."

"Okay, I do understand. Would you be leaving in two weeks or a month from now?"

"No. Today is my last day."

"Today! What about your caseload?"

"I will complete all my briefs today and make sure that all open cases have a status update on them so whoever takes them over would know exactly where to go with them."

"Richard, you know, usually it is more professional to give an employer at least a two week notice so that they can prepare."

"Yes, I do understand that, however, if it was me that was killed wouldn't you have figured it out anyway?"

"Well I expect completed briefs and an update status on everything you have before you leave the office today. Good luck to you."

"Thank you, Fletcher."

I went to my office, closed the blinds and the door behind me, turned on my iPod to Thelonious Monk and began working and stayed working not leaving until everything was completed.

Chapter 21

Despite having to have left the office at nearly 8:00 pm, I decided that I wanted to take a drive to Wellsboro, Pennsylvania and rent a lodge at Bear Mountain Resort so that I can gather my thoughts, mediate, and think about what my purpose is and what my next move in life is going to be.

When I get home, I first take Samantha out for a walk since she's been alone in the house all day, and then I pack enough clothes to last me at least three or four days. I get some dog toys and treats for Samantha and place them in another bag since she would be going with me. By the time I'm done packing and get everything in order before leaving, it is nearly quarter to ten.

Although I am a bit tired it doesn't take me long to get on the road in order to make this nearly four-hour drive. I keep my mind active and awake by thinking about the experience that I had the other day when I saw Ciana in my "dream." About two hours into my journey I start to get a bit tired, so I stop at a rest stop to get a cup of coffee and a hotdog. The coffee taste like warm colored water and the hotdog taste like cold rubber, but I consume it anyway and then get back on the road to continue onward trying to reach my destination at a reasonable hour. I speed up to about 80 miles per hour even though the speed limit is 65 unbeknownst to me that I had just passed a sitting cop squad car.

It wasn't until about a mile down the road that I see the bright flashing lights of the squad car increasing its speed behind me. Not thinking anything of it, I just keep on going maintaining my speed.

All of a sudden, I notice the squad car is right behind me with its siren blaring at me. I pull my car over to the shoulder wondering why I'm being stopped for. The spotlight shines so bright through the back window that it startles Samantha. She starts jumping around confused so, I turn around to try to calm and settle her down.

"Driver, I need you to turn off your engine and throw the key out the window with your hands up!" yelled a police officer on his loudspeaker.

What the Hell is going on here? I think to myself. I did nothing wrong. I comply with the officer and then notice three more cop cars pulling up around me.

The first police officer gets out of his car with his weapon drawn and tells me to step out of the car with my hands in the air.

"Driver, I need you to get out of your vehicle and walk backwards to me with your hands up until I tell you to stop."

I say nothing and just comply fearing that if I make any quick movement that I will be shot.

"Stop right there and kneel on the ground with your hands on your head." He tells me as I am halfway between my car and the officer's car.

"Officer, what did I do? Why did you stop me?" I ask.

"Just do as I say, and I will let you know." The officer tells me.

I comply. I notice that Samantha is very riled up now, constantly barking and jumping up and down in the back seat. I usually tie her leash onto the back of the headrest but this evening I had actually forgot about doing so. I guess I really didn't think about it since I had just figured that she would have probably slept the entire trip. As I'm knelling on the ground, Samantha leaps in the front seat and then bolts out the open driver's side door running towards me.

"SAMANTHA, NOOO! STOP!!" I yell.

POP! POP! POP!

An officer shoots and fires at Samantha hitting her three times. She goes down, makes a whimpering noise and then goes silent.

"YOU FUCKING ASSHOLE! YOU KILLED MY DOG!" I yell turning to the officer that shot her noticing that his gun is now pointed at me.

"Keep your hand on your head or you'll be next." The officer says.

Knelling on the ground with my hands on my head I'm watching the officers ravage through all my belongings in my car. No warrant, no probable cause, no reasonable suspicion. At this very moment, while I knell here and watch this debacle unfold, I finally realize my purpose.

"Where are you heading to?" a tall skinny officer with the deepest, cold blue eyes I've ever seen asks me as he takes my driver's license.

"I don't have to tell you that. What's your reason for stopping me in the first place?" I ask.

"We don't have to have a reason to stop anyone. If we are conducting an investigation and need to stop someone, we will do just that." He says to me.

His answer had infuriated me. There are so many motorists who tolerate police officers' abuse just because they don't know their rights, especially the black motorists.

"What are you talking about? You can't stop someone without probable cause." I forcefully tell him.

"Of course, we can. That's T.V. shit that you are thinking about. It doesn't work like that in real life." The officer says with a very sly look on his face.

"Do you have any drugs or weapons on you or in your car?"

Thank God I left my pistol at the house. I often keep it in my car for protection. He would of shot me first and ask questions later.

"No, I do not."

"You better tell me the truth, because we will find it and when we do, you will get in more trouble than if you just tell us the truth from the beginning."

"I just told you. There is nothing in the car."

"Why are you referring to the vehicle as, 'the car' and not saying, 'my car?' Whose car is this?"

"Maybe you should check the registration and find out for yourself."

"Do you have any current open warrants on you?"

"No."

"When was the last time you were in jail?"

"I'm not answering that question. As a matter of fact, I'm not answering any more of your questions."

"I'm just here to help you. We can arrest you just for the simple fact that you were going 80 miles per hour in a 65 mile per hour zone. So, you might want to cooperate here, or you'll be going with me in handcuffs."

"Do what you have to do then. I told you that I will not answer any more of your silly ass questions."

I notice that one of the officers who was looking in the glove compartment found my ID badge from the Public Defender's Office and notice that it showed my picture with the word "Attorney" under my name. He immediately stopped the unwarranted search and told the other officers to stop as well. All the officers' attitudes had changed drastically from being mean, disrespectful and ruthless to being overly nice and friendly.

"Hey Mr. Clayton, we apologize for any inconvenience however your car fits the description of a vehicle that was reported stolen and used in an armed robbery earlier today. We had to use every precaution possible in order to ensure our safety."

As I'm getting off of my knees the officer that was the rudest to me and killed Samantha didn't even apologize but just justified his actions and how I "fit the description" of someone who stole a similar car as mine. I knew that this was all bullshit and didn't hold back a tongue lashing.

"Are all of you cops fucking psycho or something! Now that you found out that I am an attorney and know about the law you try to make nice to me?? Shit, if I were not an attorney you would have probably tried to railroad me. How many black people do you all do this to? You fucking killed my dog!!!"

"We are very sorry sir. Your dog was charging at us, so we felt threatened. We can call Animal Control to take care of the dog's carcass if that helps. If you'd like to file a complaint here is our information." One of the officers say as he hands me a business card.

"File a complaint!?! You're goddamn fucking right I will. You better believe I'm going to do more than that. This is not going to be the last that you will hear of me."

The officers cleaned up the area and left. I just wait by Samantha's side petting her lifeless body until Animal Control shows up to take her body away and then I get back into my car still going forward towards my destination. I'm angry as hell but even more focused than I have been in a very long time.

When realizing that if I had packed my gun to bring with me I probably wouldn't be alive right now. These officers were looking for a reason to shoot. Their mentality was; shoot first and ask questions later. I now see what millions of Black males have to go through on a daily basis and why so many of them end up dead at the hands of cops. I found my purpose. My purpose is to use my legal talent and expertise to stop the injustice done to so many millions of Black Americans.

Chapter 22

I remember one day when I was a sophomore in college, me and a friend drove up to Delaware to attend a Run DMC concert that was being held on a college campus in Wilmington. As we were driving there, a cop that was behind us began to speed up and caught up to us and then pulled us over. Me and my friend didn't know what was going on and why the cop and his partner pulled us over. I was then taken out of my car and then searched and handcuffed as I was being questioned by the first officer in the backseat of the squad car. My friend stayed in my car while the second officer questioned him. At 20 years old, I was scared. I had no idea that what these cops were doing was unconstitutional and illegal. After about an hour and a half of being detained by them they released us and laughed as if they felt that we should be happy that they didn't find anything. It really is amazing what people can do to you when you don't know any better. If that scenario happened today, I would put so much litigation on them their grandchildren would still be paying their legal expenses.

It was about 2:00 in the morning by the time I reached my destination at Bear Mountain Resort, yet I have so much adrenaline in me that I am not even near being sleepy or tired. I had just realized my new purpose and I am so elated to know that this would be the venture where I make a difference: Stopping police injustice and brutality.

Long before social media brought to the forefront all the police brutality and abuse cases against those who are of minority race, the late Johnnie Cochran represented individuals such as; Haitian immigrant Abner Louima, who had been sodomized by New York City police with a Billy Club back in the 80s; Leonard Deadwyler, the black motorist who was fatally shot during a police stop in Los Angeles as he rushed his pregnant wife to the hospital, and Amadou Diallo, the unarmed African immigrant who was shot nineteen times by police officers. Johnnie Cochran's fight against injustice had brought in well over $100 million dollars in settlements during his tenure.

I open up my laptop and started to find all the stories of injustice done onto minorities, especially Black men. As I start to read over all the various cases of injustice that was brought upon by police officers against minorities, a deep feeling of contention mixed with enthusiasm started to boil deep inside the core of my heart and my soul.

I read the story of Terence Crutcher who was fatally shot in Tulsa in September of 2016 because the police officer just thought he was a "bad dude" even though his hands were raised in the air and was fully complying. That officer who killed him was fully acquitted. I read the story of Philando Castile who while driving with his girlfriend in Minnesota, was shot twice in the heart right in front of his girlfriend because he had a gun in the car even though he had a permit for it and had informed the officer of it as soon as the car was pulled over. That officer was found not guilty. I read the story of Alton Sterling who was shot by an officer a total of six times for selling CD's outside a convenience store in Baton Rouge. No charges came against the officer.

I read about Walter Scott from South Carolina, who was shot five times in the back by a police officer and how that officer tried to compromise the crime scene by trying to frame him by placing a weapon by the body. I read about Eric Harris of Tulsa who was "accidentally shot" by an officer who had supposedly mistaken his .38-caliber handgun for a stun gun. Then there was the story of Tony Robinson in Wisconsin, although unarmed, the 19-year old was shot by an officer seven times. Again, the officer faced no charges. Then there was Rumain Brisbon in Phoenix, shot by an officer because he failed to take his hands out of his pockets quick enough. The officer faced no criminal prosecution. Then 12-year old Tamir Rice from Cleveland, where an officer jumped out of his squad car and immediately shot Tamir because he was holding a toy gun. The officer was not charged. Then there was Laquan McDonald in Chicago, Michael Brown Jr. in Ferguson, and Eric Garner in New York. The list goes on and on.

This is where I need to be. I need to be in the forefront of this and change the law, change the system, change America. I believe completely and emphatically as I have ever believed anything in life that my fight is here and has just begun.

Chapter 23

It was a very nice and warm sunny day when I drove back home from spending some time in the mountains in Pennsylvania. The May air was very crisp and clear, and the good thing was that there was not a lot of people on the road as I'm driving back so I sped a little although still making sure that I didn't go too much over the speed limit.

Still enthused about starting my own practice which would be focusing mainly on civil rights and police abuse and corruption issues, I basically had no idea how I would even get started or how I would get paid for that matter. Usually cases like this are done on a contingency basis, which means that my money will only happen if I get a settlement. I'm just hoping that my little ad that I had placed online yesterday will eventually pay off.

I figure that my savings could hold me over for at least three or four months, however, if things don't come together quick enough then I may have to take on cases that I never wanted to do, like divorces or child custody cases. Those type of cases are so draining and unless a client is rich then I'd just be making pennies. I never thought that I would ever end up struggling, but then, I guess I always thought Saundra and I would always be life partners and so we would never have to struggle. I now see that I did put too much pressure on her to follow my dreams.

When I reach home, I'm very anxious and happy to see that there were already four voicemail messages on my business line. I had just placed the advertisement online yesterday, and I already have messages!

"Message Number One: 'Good Morning Mr. Clayton, this is Jeremiah Scott. I would like to talk to you about something if you are available.'"

Jeremiah Scott? I wonder why he's calling me. I really hope that he is not in any trouble again. I no longer do criminal defense, so I really won't be able to help him this time.

"Message Number Two: 'Hi Mr. Clayton, this is Jeremiah Scott again. I really need to speak with you.'"

"Message Number Three: 'Hey Mr. Clayton, Jeremiah here. Sorry to bother you again, I just want to ask you something. I guess I'll just try to reach you tomorrow. Thanks Mr. Clayton.'"

"Message Number Four: 'Good evening Mr. Clayton. My name is Robert Chase."

Great! Someone other than Jeremiah!

The message continues: "I would like to discuss a potential case with you. I know that you are probably a very busy person, so I will try you back tomorrow morning in order to see if my wife and I can come into your office to discuss a situation regarding our son Trevor."

I have no idea what Jeremiah wants but I guess the good news is that I just might have a new client.

***

Trevor Chase was driving home to Maryland from his college which is located in Georgia, for summer break and had been on the road all night. The eleven-hour drive started to take a toll on his body by the time he reached Maryland at 1:30 in the morning. And of course, it didn't help that he didn't get much sleep the night before since he had partied hard with his fraternity brothers his last day on campus. When Trevor was on Interstate 95 North only about 35 minutes from his parents' house in Baltimore, his eyes were so heavy that it was very hard for him to stay awake, but he wanted to push through since he was so close to home.

A Maryland State police officer notices Trevor's car weaving between lanes and decided to pull him over since the officer didn't know whether the driver was intoxicated, or drug induced. Trevor pulls over his little blue Honda Civic and squints his bloodshot eyes as the officer's flashlight shines in his face. The officer requests Trevor's license and registration with a very loud and firm voice as Trevor seemed to be in a daze. Trevor slowly finds the documents and hands them over to the officer. As the officer goes back inside of his squad car to check out Trevor's license and registration, he notices that Trevor's car starts to move backwards rapidly. The officer then jumps out of his car and yells for the driver to stop his vehicle however the car continues to swiftly move backwards as if charging to hit the squad car. The officer then pulls out his service weapon and fires it into the moving car. The officer fires off a total of sixteen rounds into the vehicle emptying the clip of his service weapon. Thirteen of those bullets hit Trevor, killing him.

When this story came to light, everyone was extremely angry over the police officer's actions. The officer was never charged of any type of recklessness because he had believed that Trevor was under the influence of some type of narcotic, possibly PCP and aggressively tried to ram his vehicle into the officer's squad car. The State believed the officer's account of what happened and believed the officer's actions were justified so it was written up as the officer carrying out his duties as a police officer. No one else had believed the officer however, and because there were no witnesses around, it couldn't be disputed. Trevor's parents were distraught and knew that he didn't use drugs and his friends collaborated that statement.

When the State chose not to make the police officer accountable for the death of Trevor his parents came to my home/office to take civil action against the police officer and the State of Maryland. If the State wasn't going to have the officer brought up on criminal charges and have him put in jail, then we are going to make the State pay financially.

"Good afternoon, Mr. and Mrs. Chase." I say as I extend my hand to shake theirs and take them to the den in my house. "I am really sorry for your loss and am very interested in taking on this case."

"Good afternoon, Mr. Clayton. Thank you for helping us." Mr. Chase says.

"I assume that you reached me because you saw my recent ad that I had posted online, may I ask though, why you chose me from other attorneys?" I ask.

"We actually have heard of you before. We know that you were once a public defender here in Baltimore City and was consider one of the best. We learned of this when we heard of your story on the news a few months ago about the death of your daughter. We were taken aback when it was mentioned that the man who you had recently represented was the one who accidentally killed your daughter. We were so sorry to hear about your tragedy." Mrs. Chase stated.

When Mrs. Chase made that comment I started to feel a wave of emotion start to build up in my stomach again which made me feel a bit nauseated. I closed my eyes for a moment and took a deep breath in order to hold my composure.

"Yes, well thank you. I'm sorry about your tragedy as well." I say quickly trying to move on.

"We saw in your ad that you now fight for civil rights and police brutality, and we wanted to see if you would be able to help us." stated Mr. Chase.

"The State is removing themselves from any liability and is stating that the officer acted appropriately and was just in his actions. Now I will say this, even if your son was drug induced and he did ram his car into the police car, I do believe that the officer had used excessive force in order to subdue him. Shooting into a vehicle sixteen times is very excessive. The officer knew that there was no one else in the car and I am sure he knew that your son was unarmed." I tell them.

"Trevor wasn't into drugs!" Mrs. Chase exclaims forcefully.

"I understand that he may not have been on any drugs, however, we just have to be prepared just in case. Once we get the toxicology report we can be certain, however, please do not be alarmed if something might have been found in his blood stream. He is a Junior in college, sometimes things happen." I tell her.

"Would you be able to get the dash cam footage from the police car? We had asked to see it however we were told that we couldn't since no charges were brought on the officer and it was considered confidential." stated Mr. Chase.

"Confidential?!? That's hogwash. The Freedom of Information Act allows you to obtain that footage. It's the law. You have a right to it. I will probably have to subpoena it." I tell him.

"How much do we have to put down in order for you to start on our case?" asked Mr. Chase.

"Actually, this is what is called a contingency case. I only get money if we win a settlement. If we win a settlement, I will get fifteen percent plus all my expenses that I had paid out." I tell him.

"Oh, I see. So how does this work? Where do we start?" asked Mr. Chase.

"Well we are starting right now, so I need to know everything about Trevor, whether it's good or bad. The State is going to try to get whatever dirt they can get on him, so I need to know everything. I don't want any surprises. I am also going to speak to all of his friends that he may have had or anyone one he was associated with. I want to know his grades in school and his credits. Anything that you can think of, I need for you to give to me. Understand?" I ask.

"Yes." Mrs. Chase says and then continues. "Well, he attended Wailer College in Georgia and carried a 3.2 grade point average. He was on the basketball team there and I believe that he joined a fraternity. I just can't remember the name of it right now, but we can find out and then let you know. He had a girlfriend that we met last Thanksgiving when he brought her over to the house for Thanksgiving dinner who attends the school as well. Her name is Sarah and lives down there in Georgia."

"Do you know what part of Georgia that she resides in?" I ask.

"I believe that it is Atlanta. She called us when she didn't hear from him for several days when he was supposed to be back. She was up here for the funeral three weeks ago."

"Do you have a list of people who attended Trevor's funeral?"

"Well, we did have a condolence registry that people signed when they came into the church where we held the funeral at, but I don't think everyone who was there signed it"

"I'm going to need that. I'm also going to need the names and numbers of any of his close friends or associates, a copy of his college transcripts and even a copy of his driving record. I need to know everything, even if he had any speeding or parking tickets."

"Why would you need all this information about him? It was the police officer's fault; shouldn't it be him that we look at?" Mr. Chase asks.

"Of course, I will find a bunch of information on the officer as well, however, the State is going to try and muddy up your son's character. They are going to try to prove that the police officer was right and was justified in his actions." I tell him. "I must tell you, though, you both may be called up to the stand as well. Is there anything that I should know?"

"Well I do have a record." stated Mr. Chase.

"Ok, tell me about it."

"Well when I was 23 years old, I was arrested and charged with possession of a CDS."

"Ok, what was the controlled dangerous substance you were arrested for?"

"It was cocaine."

"What was the outcome?" I ask.

"I was convicted and did three years in prison. I was charged with distribution, manufacturing, and possession and was looking at 24 years in prison, but it was brought down to a simple possession through a plea agreement."

"How old are you now?"

"I am 51."

"Since then have you been in any trouble with the law?

"No, I have not. I am a law-abiding citizen. I don't even get any speeding or parking tickets. I just go to work and take care of my family. Do you think that my past will come up?"

"To be quite honest with you, I don't know. Although that happened well over 25 years ago, the State might try to bring up anything that they can."

"What do you do for a living?"

"I work for the Post Office as a sorter. Been working there for twenty-three years."

"How about you, Mrs. Chase? Is there anything that I should know about?"

"No, aside from a couple of speeding tickets, I have never broken the law." She replied.

"What do you do for a living?"

"I work for the post office too. That's how Robert and I met." Stated Mrs. Chase.

"Now what can we expect? How does this work?" asked Mr. Chase.

"Well I am going to start off by filing a civil suit for wrongful death against the State and the police department in the Federal Court since there was a constitutional violation involved and will sue for compensatory and punitive damages." I tell them.

"Now being that we will be trying a civil case in the federal court, this is much different than criminal court. Whereas in criminal court the State must prove 'beyond a reasonable doubt,' civil courts require something called, a 'preponderance of the evidence' when determining liability in civil cases. Actually, federal law requires a slightly higher burden of proof; 'clear and convincing evidence,' for claims of civil rights violations. Also, a jury doesn't need to have a unanimous decision but just a majority"

"Are we going to sue the police officer as well?" Mr. Chase asks.

"Police officers generally have broad powers to carry out their duties. In fact, police officers are usually immune from lawsuits for the performance of their jobs unless willful, unreasonable conduct is demonstrated. Mere negligence, the failure to exercise due care, is not enough to create liability. This is the position that the State is taking.

Now, if things really went the way we think it went down, we may have recourse through federal and state laws. There is a statute known as Section 1983 within Title 42 of the United States Code, which is the primary civil rights law victims of police misconduct rely upon. Just a little history on it; this law was originally passed as part of the Civil Rights Act of

1871 and was intended to curb oppressive conduct by government and private individual participating in vigilante groups, such as the Ku Klux Klan. Section 1983 makes it unlawful for anyone acting under the authority of state law to deprive another person of his or her rights under the Constitution or federal law, which would include unreasonable or excessive force by police officers."

"What would constitute excessive force?" asked Mrs. Chase.

"Excessive force refers to situations where government officials legally entitled to use force exceed the minimum amount necessary to diffuse an incident or to protect themselves or others from harm. The constitutional right to be free from excessive force is found in the reasonable search and seizure requirement of the Fourth Amendment and the prohibition on cruel and unusual punishment in the Eight Amendment."

"How much are we going to sue for?" Mr. Chase asks.

"Well let me let you know that damages and settlement amounts can vary quite a bit from one jurisdiction to the next. There have been settlements as low as seventy-five hundred dollars, however, there have been some settlements as high as 8.5 million dollars. I figure in this case we will go for somewhere in the ballpark from three to five million dollars." I tell them.

"Ok, but what if we lose. The police officer would have gotten away with it and Trevor's death would be in vain." Mrs. Chase states.

"Look, I know that there is really no amount of money that will replace your son, but we need the State to know their wrongdoing and have them think twice before doing something like this again. If we lose, at least we have made a dent in the system. This is not just about money, it's also about making change."

"Well Mr. Clayton, we do trust you and will follow what you say."

"Great! Then let the games begin."

Chapter 24

"Hello, Richard Clayton here." I say as I answer the ringing business phone in my den.

"Hi Mr. Clayton, this is Jeremiah Scott."

"Hi Jeremiah, I heard your previous messages, is everything ok?"

"Yes, for the most part. I would like to ask you a question though if you have a few minutes to talk."

"Yes, sure. Shoot."

"Well, first I'd like to say thank you for always seeming to believe in me. I greatly appreciate that. Your belief in me has inspired me in ways that I couldn't image. You seemed to have always believed in me even from the first day that we met at the jail. Why is that?"

"Jeremiah, believe it or not, you are not too much different than me. I have always seen the potential that you have in yourself, you just needed the right guidance to get it out of you. Just because I am an attorney doesn't mean that I had always been guided and have always done the right things in my past."

"Oh really? What do you mean?"

"Well when I was about 21-years old, I too had gotten into trouble with the law. When I was in college, I'd hang around some guys in the neighborhood that didn't do much with their lives except hang out all day long and smoke or sold weed. Of course, being young, I really didn't make the best decisions and really thought that these guys were my friends, so although I was in school, I didn't want them to think that I wasn't down with them. I ended up delivering a package to some guy that they didn't really know but thought that I would be the best person to deliver it to him since it was supposed to be delivered to him on the college campus that I was going to. Turns out that this package was about a quarter of a pound of marijuana and the guy that I delivered the package to was an undercover cop."

"Oh snap! Wow, so what happened?"

"Well I got arrested. That's what happened."

"Seriously!"

"Yup! It wasn't right away though. After I gave the package to the undercover cop he asked me if I could get another package for him in a couple of days and he would pay me a lot more money if I got him a pound."

"Did you get it for him?"

"I was going to at first, but my so-called friends told me that he could have been an undercover cop and they told me not to give him anything else and of course, they thought the whole situation was very funny and didn't take it seriously. I didn't think it was funny at all because I had already given the man a quarter of a pound of marijuana so I'm thinking that I'm already in trouble, but of course, my so-called friends tell me not to worry because it would be his word against my word and besides, he would have arrested me already if he had anything on me."

"So, what happened?"

"Well the day that I was supposed to meet him to give him the pound of marijuana I avoided all contact with him. Back then we didn't have cell phones like the way we have them today, however, we did have pagers. He kept beeping my pager, but I kept ignoring it. About 10:00 at night as I'm thinking that I'm in the clear I hear the front door of my apartment smash inward and these men wearing what looked like black Ninja suits with their faces covered come charging at me with their guns pointed at my head yelling for me to get down on the floor. Of course, I complied with their orders thinking that I was getting robbed. When they strap my hands behind my back using plastic handcuffs and pulled me up into a sitting position, I turned my head and recognized an officer who worked on the university's campus and remembered that he was also a part of the narcotics task force. They searched my apartment looking for the pound of marijuana or anything they could find but never got anything because I didn't have anything. I thought that they were going to release me, however, my so-called friends were wrong. They could still charge me for what I gave the undercover officer that first time, and of course, they did."

"Wow! That is something!"

"When they took me to jail, they set a fifty-thousand-dollar bond on me. Six months later I went to trial for possession and distribution of a schedule two drug and was looking at about 10 years in prison. Do you know what was the only thing that saved me?"

"No, what?"

"My intelligence. The judge saw that I was very intelligent but had made a very bad decision and offered me a plea agreement. The plea agreement was to drop the charge down to a misdemeanor with a 12-month jail sentence and four years' probation."

"So, you still had to stay in jail longer?"

"Yes, but it was a lot better than 10 years in prison and coming out as a convicted felon which was what I was originally facing. And because the judge knew that I was in college he allowed me to continue with school by going to class in the day and then going back to the jail at night."

"Wow, that's really something. I would never have guessed that you've been through something like that."

"The judge did that because he believed in me. Had he not seen my potential I would have been just like every other black male in that jail who committed a crime. I would have had a guaranteed trip to prison. So, you see, that is what I've seen in you. Your potential for something better."

"Thank you for seeing that in me, Mr. Clayton."

"You are welcome. If there is anything else that I can do for you, please let me know."

"Well, now that you mention it, there is something else."

"What's going on?"

"Well I was wondering if I could volunteer with you at the public defender's office. I think that I want to be an attorney too, just like you, helping people."

"Well, Jeremiah, I actually no longer work at the public defender's office, however, I can give you a choice though. I can either make some phone calls and pull some strings at the public defender's office to get you there so that you can volunteer with one of my former colleagues or I can bring you on here with me at my new practice that I am starting. Although at the public defender's office you will get an unlimited supply of work and experience, I can give you more hands-on experience and train you to be a paralegal.

Which would you like for me to do?"

"Well Mr. Clayton, I would rather work with you. I want to learn from you and if possible, want you to be a mentor to me."

"Well you got it! Can you start tomorrow?"

"Absolutely!" Jeremiah exclaimed.

"Great, then meet me at the Starbucks on the corner of Howard and Franklin streets by 9:00 a.m. tomorrow morning and we'll jump right into it. I'll even buy you a cup of coffee."

"I don't drink coffee, but tea would be good."

"Cool, then tea it is. See you tomorrow, Jeremiah."

"Okay, Mr. Clayton. Thanks for everything."

"You are certainly welcome." I say.

Chapter 25

It was pouring rain when I finally get to the Starbucks at the corner of Howard and Franklin streets, however luckily, I was still about ten minutes early. As I stepped inside to look for a table that Jeremiah and I can sit at to discuss my new case, I noticed that Jeremiah was already here at a table in the back and was prepared to start working with his pen and pad ready to get started.

"Hey Jeremiah! You're here already? When did you get here?" I asked.

"Oh, I got here at about 8:30. I just wanted to make sure that I was on time so we can get started right away."

"Wow, I'm really impressed. You are really serious about this." I tell him.

"Yes I am. I want to be a lawyer some day and I am willing to start from the ground up and do whatever it takes."

"Well with that work ethic you will definitely become one. A very good one at that."

"Thanks, Mr. Clayton."

"What kind of tea can I get you?"

"Regular tea I guess."

"How about a Chai Latte'"

"Sure, I guess. Is it tea?"

"It's good. Trust me." I tell him.

"Okay, I'll try it."

"Cool." I say as I'm walking to the counter to order our drinks.

I get back to our table about 10 minutes later and hand him his Chai tea.

"Well, how is it?" I ask as he takes a sip.

"Pretty darn good." He says smiling.

"Great. Well, let's begin. The case that I am working on is a police brutality and obsessive use of force which caused a death. Did you hear about the incident of the young man who was travelling back home from his college and a police officer ended up shooting at him sixteen times?"

"Yes, I heard about that case. They said that the guy was on drugs and ended up trying to ram the officer's car, but a lot of people don't believe it."

"What do you believe?"

"Honestly, I don't believe what the officer said either. It just didn't make sense to me because I don't see why the guy would want to ram the police car. If anything, why wouldn't he just drive forward if he wanted to get away?"

"That is very good deductive reasoning. That is what we are going to find out. We need to find out why the vehicle was moving backwards and what was his state of mind during the stop."

"How are we going to find out what his state of mind was now that he is dead?"

"Well we are going to get access to all the videos that we can. We are going to try to get the dash camera as well as the officer's vest cam. They are not trying to release that footage to us, but we could end up getting a subpoena in order to force them to do so. Also, we are going to contact all the people that he was last in contact with. His parents have given me his cell phone, so we are going to go through the phone and find out who he was corresponding with then contact them. His friends should be able to tell us his state of mind."

"Oh, ok."

"We are also going to get information on the police officer who stopped him. We'll do a Google search on him as well as search multiple forms of social media.

I will show you different databases that are not in the public domain where you can look anybody up and get thorough information on them. Make sure that you use these databases for the victim as well. We don't want any surprises when we go to trial."

"Okay. Will we be working in here every day?"

"No, we will be working out of my home office. Everything that we need will be there. I am going to write down the address here on this paper and we can meet there around 10:00 a.m. tomorrow morning, that way I can stop by the courthouse and file our complaint. Actually, make it 11:00 a.m., I may not make it back by 10. Also, one of the things that we must do is to go exactly where the incident took place. We need to visualize the incident and we need to see if it is possible that the car could have just rolled backwards instead of the claim that it was reversed."

"Ok, I can start with his cell phone now. I'll call up his friends and let you know what the outcome is when we meet tomorrow at your office."

"Start out with his girlfriend, her name is Sarah. I'm pretty sure that she probably was the last person he was with before he left Georgia. Also, I need you to check out his social media accounts. See what was posted by him and about him."

"Okay, got it!"

"Great! I'll see you tomorrow at 11:00, then."

"Okay, see you then."

Chapter 26

IN THE UNITED STATES DISTRICT COURT FOR THE DISTRICT OF MARYLAND, I start to type.

Robert Chase, Belinda Chase, Trevor Chase, et el, plaintiffs versus Ronald Rand, PFC and the Maryland State Police, Defendants. CIVIL RIGHTS COMPLAINT FOR TRIAL BY JURY. Plaintiffs Robert Chase, Belinda Chase, and Trevor Chase, by and through their attorney, the Law Office of Richard Clayton, complains against their Defendants, Ronald Rand, and the Maryland State Police requests trial by Jury as follows: 1. This is an action brought on by Mr. Robert Chase and Mrs. Belinda Chase, the parents of Trevor Chase, who was an African-American college student, to vindicate profound deprivations of his constitutional rights by race-based police brutality. 2. On May 10th of the current year, Plaintiff Trevor Chase, then 21 years old, was stopped by Maryland State police in a traffic stop for allegedly weaving his vehicle on Interstate 95. 3. During the course of this stop, Trevor Chase was shot and killed by officer, Private First-Class Ronald Rand, who had unloaded his weapon into Chase's car landing thirteen of the sixteen bullets into Chase's body.

It took me up until about 3:00 in the morning to finally finish this thirty-seven-page civil rights complaint that I will file later today at the federal courthouse in downtown Baltimore. I wanted to make sure the complaint would be complete and filed before Jeremiah comes to the home/office to give me any information that he may have learned.

When the time finally came to file the complaint in the courthouse, I look over the document one more time before handing it over to the court clerk for filing, making sure that all the information in the complaint is correct and nothing is omitted. When everything looked okay, I hand it over to the clerk and wait to be given a case number.

When the clerk takes the document, she looks it over and hesitates for a few minutes with a dismayed look on her face.

"Is there something wrong?" I ask.

"I'm sorry, I'm just making sure that you are filing this case in the right courthouse." She responds.

"Well, I'm pretty sure that this is in the right courthouse. This is a civil rights case involving violations of the Constitution. This Court does have jurisdiction.

"I do agree that this type of case would be filed in the federal court however because the incident happened on Interstate 95, depending on the exact location it might have to be filed at the Greenbelt federal court location. Let me ask my supervisor and get back with you in a second."

"Ok, no problem." I say although I was clearly annoyed at this problem.

She finally comes back to me about ten minutes later letting me know what I already knew, that this courthouse does hold jurisdiction, but I pleasantly thank her for double checking, pay the $400 filing fee, and then go on my merry way.

By the time I reach home, Jeremiah is already at my door waiting to come in. I am really impressed with his ambition, drive, and timeliness.

"Hey Jeremiah, how are you today?"

"I'm good Mr. Clayton. I found out some information from my phone calls yesterday."

"Great! What did you find out?"

"Well, Trevor was at a party the night before and he did drink some alcohol and smoked a little weed, however, but the time he left to go to Maryland, his best friend said that he was fine. He left around 3:00 in the afternoon which was pretty late to leave Atlanta knowing it is about a 10-hour drive. However, his friend said that Trevor made sure that he would be okay to drive. His girlfriend also had told me the same thing."

"That's good to know. If anything comes back in the toxicology report regarding any type of substance, at least we will be prepared. Did you ask if they would be willing to testify in court?"

"Yes, I did ask everyone. They all are willing to come to court."

"Great!" I say clearly very excited. "Let's take a drive."

"Where to?"

"We are going to go to the exact location of where the traffic stop and the shooting took place."

It took us a little while to find the exact location of where the incident took place. When we finally found it, I had parked my car right where the police officer had his car parked. I could still actually see the broken glass and shard metal from Trevor's blue car.

As Jeremiah and I stand in front of my car, we analyze the area. The first thing that we notice is the upward slant of the road. There is about a thirty-five-degree upward slant. It is interesting how I never really notice any type of upward or downward slant in the road as I take this highway. For some reason, I always thought that the highway was 100% flat the entire way. I guess we don't really think about slants when travelling at 75 or 80 miles per hour. Looking at this slant, I can see how a car could roll backwards.

We decided to test the "roll-back" theory and place my car where Trevor's car was when he first got pulled over.

"Hey Jeremiah, sit in the driver's seat and when I tell you to, release the brake by lifting your foot off of the pedal." I tell him.

"Okay."

I stand back where the police car was and then tell Jeremiah to release the brake.

"Release the break now, Jeremiah." I shout to him.

As soon as he takes his foot off of the brake pedal, the car starts to roll backwards towards me, and increases in speed.

"Ok, stop the car!"

Jeremiah complies and the car halts.

"Place it back in the initial position. This time I want to time the speed." I tell Jeremiah.

Once Jeremiah puts the car back in the spot, he releases the break again and I start to document the speed.

"Wow, from Trevor's position to the officer's position took the car less than three seconds. The car goes pretty swiftly backwards."

"So, case solved, right?! This right here proves that he didn't reverse back on purpose."

"Well, it's not going to be that easy. Just because we are on a slight incline doesn't mean that he didn't reverse his car to try to hit the officer."

"Hey Mr. Clayton, do you see that building over there on the other side of the highway?" Jeremiah says pointing to a ten-story building which was diagonal to where we were standing. "Do you think that they might have some cameras that could have possibly taken aim towards this side of the highway?"

"You know, that's not a bad question. You might be onto something. Well, it doesn't hurt to find out." I tell him.

It takes us a little while until we get to the building on the other side of the highway. We had to first drive up two miles until the next exit allowed us to take the ramp to the other side and then when we were on I-95 south, we had to drive down for about four miles and then go through an area with plenty of back streets in order to find this building since there was no direct way of getting there.

When we get to the building we first find the property management office so that we can ask permission to go to the security office to see if we can view their video tapes.

"Hello, ma'am, are you the building manager?" I ask

"Yes, I am. How can I help you?" She asks in a way as if she did something wrong.

"My name is Richard Clayton and this is my assistant Jeremiah Scott. I am an attorney representing the parents of the slain African American college kid who was gunned down by a police officer on I-95 a few weeks ago."

"Ah, yes. I heard about that story on the news. How can I help you?" she asks.

"Well, I know that this is a long shot request but is there any way that I could review your outside security footage which faces the highway."

"Absolutely! Do you think that you may find something on it?" she responds ecstatically.

"We're really not too sure." I tell her.

She takes us down to the security room which is located in the basement of the building and points to the monitors of the cameras which face the highway.

"These three monitors points to that area. Security will give you that night's footage however for whatever reason it's only in one-hour increments, so you may have to sit through it for a while before seeing the scene that you are searching for."

"It's cool." I tell her. "Thank you very much for your assistance. Jeremiah you watch the footage on this monitor, and I will watch it on these two other monitors.

It's not until about 45 minutes in, we find the police stop that we were looking for.

"Hey Mr. Clayton! Look! It's right here!" Jeremiah says to me.

I turn to Jeremiah's monitor and stare at the incident very intently. The police car's flashing lights are on, while Trevor's car pulls over. The police officer walks up to Trevor's car, gets information, and then nonchalantly walks back to his car and then gets into his car. Moments later the car goes backwards, and then the officer jumps out of his car yelling as he draws his weapon. The car continues to roll backwards swiftly and with the officer's gun still drawn, he starts firing continuously.

"Jeremiah, look! Do you notice what I notice?" I say enthusiastically.

"I'm not sure. What do you notice?" he asks.

"Look at the car's back lights. First of all, there are no white reverse lights on. Second, the red break lights had dimmed. This means that he took his foot off of the brake pedal. So, he had to have rolled backwards as oppose to erratically or aggressively reverse backwards."

"This could be our ticket right here, right?." Jeremiah says.

"Yeah, possibly but it's not guaranteed. Can I get a copy of this footage?" I ask the security personal.

"Sure, I'll make a copy and place it on this flash drive for you." A security guard tells me.

"Thanks sir, you've helped up tremendously!" I tell the security guard.

"Hey Jeremiah, let's get some lunch and then head back to the office" I say enthusiastically. "What would you like to eat?"

"How about roast beef?"

"Cool, we had passed an Arby's on our way over here, that would be a good place to rest, eat, and chat."

"Sounds good to me, Mr. Clayton. Thanks."

Chapter 27

I have been constantly working very late ever since I had started on this case, so one can imagine my frustration when at 6:00 a.m. this morning, the doorbell rings. I hurry to put on a robe to see who is at my front door.

"Who is it?" I say yelling through the door before opening it up.

"Councilman Raymond Watts." The voice says.

Raymond Watts?! What the hell is he doing here? I mumble to myself as I open the door.

"Good morning, Councilman. What's going on? What can I do for you?" I ask.

"Good morning Mr. Clayton. I'm sorry for disturbing you so early but I didn't have your phone number. I got your address off the program from your daughter's funeral, so I just thought that I would stop by before you got too busy."

"Ok, well come in. What can I do for you?"

"Well it's actually what I can do for you."

"Ok... what are you saying?"

"I hear that you are representing the Chase case. It was such a tragedy what that police officer did to Trevor and yet he is still on the street without any repercussions. What I would like to do is perform a peaceful day long demonstration protest where about 100 to 200 protestors would walk the 30-mile journey from the federal courthouse in downtown Baltimore to the Maryland State Capitol building in downtown Annapolis. Doing this could bring national attention and awareness, and possibly change laws. I want you to come and lead the demonstration with me. I believe that if you would do this it would have an even more powerful impact because not only are you the one who is fighting against the State police however you have unfortunately experienced the tragedy of a death of a child as well."

Death of a child as well? What is this idiot talking about? My daughter wasn't killed by a police officer she was killed by one of us. He is such an opportunist. I can't believe that he is using my dead daughter and the death of Trevor for political gain. Some people will do anything for political advantage.

"Councilman, I do see what you are trying to do, and I do get the point that you are trying to make, however, for me to do a demonstration like that would not be a very good idea. Doing something like that could taint a jury. I must be as focused as possible and not hurt myself or the credibility of the case by protesting. God forbid if a peaceful demonstration got out of hand and turned into riots like it did at the Freddie Grey protest. Something like that would hurt the case. Councilman, if you wish to protest like that I do wish you much success in doing so, however, as counsel on this case, I unfortunately cannot join the demonstration. I do hope that you understand."

"I do understand your rationale for your decision; however, wouldn't you think that the more people who know and get frustrated with the system the more we would be able to make a difference for change?" states the Councilman.

"I can agree with you and that is why I am not knocking what you are trying to do, however, for me being involved with the case the way that I am, unfortunately, I cannot partake in your demonstration right now. Besides that, I'm not really sure that just protesting is really the right answer anyway. I think African Americans should study and learn the law so they can know their rights. I think that should be the message that politicians such as yourself should be telling these young black folks. Get them to learn the law. At the very least, knowing what their rights are."

"I can agree with you, Mr. Clayton, however, it starts with protesting in order for our law-makers to make a change in the law. They should adhere to the American people whether Black, White, Latino, Asian, or Native American. That is their job, to listen to the American people."

"Counselman, I'm 46 years old. I honestly have never seen protesting really make a difference. The difference has always been made when someone learns the law and then infiltrates it by becoming a member of some form of political office. You are a politician, so you know how an idea becomes a law. Leading a protest only gets you votes, not policy."

"You think that I only do this for votes? You think that I am some kind of opportunists? I resent that remark. I really do care about our people, that is why I became a politician, to make a change and a difference." Counselman says to me clearly annoyed.

"No, I'm not saying that at all. What I am saying is that the law is a weapon that we can use. Just like they use it on us, we can use it back on them. If you were to ask a young person today about The Black Panther Party, he would probably think that it was an after-party that was thrown after the viewing of Marvel's superhero movie, The Black Panther. They probably wouldn't know that it was a political organization founded by Bobby Seale and Huey Newton in the 60s and its core practice was to learn the law, especially the Second Amendment, and how to use it as a weapon against their oppressors. This is what we need to teach our citizens, our black people, especially our youths. They need to not be afraid of going to court and going up against a police officer because they know their rights."

"I understand what you are saying, however, I still believe in demonstrating our frustrations. We need to let them know that we will stand up and fight. However, I do agree with you as well. Although we must stand up and fight, in order for us to fight, we must learn the law." He states.

"Yes, indeed." I say as I extend my hand to shake his in agreement.

"Well it was a pleasure speaking with you, Mr. Clayton. I support you in your fight and if there is anything that I can do to help you please don't hesitate to call me." He says as he hands his business card to me.

"Thank you. I'll definitely hold onto your card and keep you in mind." I say. "Have a good day councilman."

"You too, Mr. Clayton."

Chapter 28

One hundred and fifty thousand dollars. One hundred and fifty thousand dollars. I kept mulling that number over and over in my head. That is the amount that the State is willing to pay for shooting and killing an innocent unarmed black man. One hundred and fifty thousand dollars. After taxes and my fees, the Chase family would probably net about roughly a cool ninety thousand dollars.

I tell Mr. and Mrs. Chase about the States offer in the hopes that they would decide not to take it but of course I say nothing because I cannot coerce them in any way.

"This case is not about money; this is a case about human dignity. No amount of money could ever bring our son back. However, with that amount of money it doesn't hurt them in any way. We need to have them hurt so much that the State would give better training to police officers and they would think twice about their actions. One hundred and fifty thousand dollars will not do it." Mrs. Chase yells out.

"Honey, you even said it yourself. This case is not about money. No amount of money will bring our son back. I think that we should take the money and move on." Mr. Chase says to his wife.

"Mr. Clayton, I really can't bring myself to accepting that settlement. Trevor was the only person in both mine and Robert's family to go to college. He was not only accepted but had gotten both an athletic scholarship and an academic scholarship which was paying his full way through school. Trevor was a miracle from God. The officer is still working as if nothing ever happened. The State needs to pay." explains Mrs. Chase.

"I understand. Unfortunately, I can't tell you to take the settlement or not. It is the both of your decision; however, I will tell you that if you decide not to take the settlement, I promise you both that I will fight my darn best in this lawsuit. I cannot tell you that we will win, but I can tell you that no matter what, we will make a change." I tell them.

"I really don't know about this. One hundred and fifty thousand is a lot of money. If we don't take it, we could end up with nothing. We are still paying for Trevor's funeral even now. No one has helped us with that expense." says Mr. Chase.

"I understand your dilemma." I tell Mr. Chase.

"Well, I love my wife more than anything in this world. I will support her decision no matter what. If she says we fight, then we fight. We will fight to the end. That is what our vows are all about. Sticking together through thick and through thin no matter what the issue is. Win or lose, we'll still be together." Mr. Chase says.

Although I couldn't help feeling a bit envious regarding their marriage, wishing that Saundra and I had that same connection, I felt more encourage than I have ever felt with any case in my life. I knew at that moment that I would fight till the end as well. If there was ever a case or a mission that I had to do, it was this one.

Mr. Chase then looked in his wife's eyes with the most passionate and endearing look that I have ever seen anyone do to another person and then he kissed her ever so passionately and effortlessly.

"We are going forward, Mr. Clayton. We are going to fight." She says very calmly as she still stares in her husband's eyes.

"Okay then. I am going to subpoena the police officer's body cam as well as the dash cam, and I am going to start gathering character witnesses, so if you have the names and numbers of those who you think would be good character witnesses then make sure that you let me know so that I can interview them."

"Okay, we'll do that. Thank you, Mr. Clayton."

"You are welcome. I thank you both as well. You gave me back my purpose."

Chapter 29

"Hey Mr. Clayton, this just came in the mail today. It's from the Office of the Chief Medical Examiner." Jeremiah tells me.

"It must be the toxicology report from the autopsy for Trevor Chase." I tell him as I take it from him and open it up.

"Positive for marijuana and amphetamine." I say, clearly a bit miffed. "The state is definitely going to have a field day with that information."

"Oh, wow. How does everything else look?" asks Jeremiah.

"Everything else is fine. I just know that they are going to juice the marijuana and amphetamine thing as much as they can. That explains the reason why they came up with that amount for a settlement. Pass me the blue flash drive on the desk. It holds the dash and body cam videos. We need to look at them."

"Ok, well hopefully we can prove what we saw on the video that the building's camera had showed us." Jeremiah says as he hands me the flash drive.

"Let's watch the body camera footage first. This will tell us Trevor's state of mind during the stop."

[Trevor: Hey officer, what's up?

Officer: Good morning, I am fitted with a body cam, so all conversation and actions are being recorded. I need your driver's license and your car registration.

Trevor: Um, sir, can you tell me why I was pulled over for?

Officer: I'll tell you after you give me your driver's license and your car registration.

Trevor: I need a minute to get them, officer. – -- Here you go. So, can you tell me now why I was pulled over?

Officer: Have you been drinking?

Trevor: No.

Officer: Have you taken any type of drugs whether illegal or prescription?

Trevor: No!

Officer: I clocked you at 80 miles per hour and also notice that you were weaving the lanes. Why are your eyes bloodshot and your speech slurred?

Trevor: I had been driving for about ten hours from Atlanta, so I'm extremely tired.

Officer: Do you have any drugs or weapons in the vehicle?

Trevor: What? No!

Officer: You are very fidgety which makes me think that you are either hiding something in the car or you are under the influence of a narcotic or alcohol.

Trevor: What the hell! I'm not hiding shit, I'm just super sleepy.

Officer: Then you won't mind if I do a quick little search of the vehicle do you?

Trevor: Yes, I do mind. No, you can't search my car.

Officer: Look, all I have to do is to call for an officer to bring a dog here to walk around your vehicle and if the K-9 alerts me to let me know that something is in the vehicle I will let the judge and the prosecutor know of your lack of cooperation. At least if you tell me now, I can be more lenient on you.

Trevor: Go right ahead then. Call a dog unit here. I'm not going to allow you to search my car.

Officer: (squeezing the button of his radio attached to his collar) Requesting backup. Possible 10-50 or 10-51, need a K-9 unit.

Officer: Wait here.

Trevor: I'm not going anywhere.

Officer goes into his car and inputs information into the computer. Approximately 8 minutes later, Trevor's car is seen going backwards. Officer then jumps out of his vehicle with weapon drawn.

Officer: STOP YOUR VEHICLE! STOP YOUR VEHICLE! STOP NOW! STOP!

POW! POW! POW! POW! POW! POW! POW! POW! POW! POW! POW! POW! POW! POW! POW! POW!

Officer: (speaking into his radio) 10-57, shots fired! Shots fired! Possible 10-53.]

"Wow, that was really intense Mr. Clayton." Jeremiah says

"Yeah, it was." I tell him as I click off the bodycam footage and then click on the file from the dashcam.

The dashcam footage starts as soon as the flashing emergency lights turn on, so we are unable to see if Trevor's car was actually weaving lanes. We fast forwarded the video to the moment the vehicle moves towards the squad car.

"Well would you look at that." I say enthusiastically. "Not only does it show that the car rolled backwards but look at Trevor's head. Do you see his head tilts back and then to the right? He fell asleep! Look! His head goes back and then to the right, and then the back lights dim, which indicates that his foot was lifted from the brake pedal."

"Wow! That is probably why he didn't stop the car.

He was asleep and didn't hear the officer. Oh my God." Jeremiah says in a very stunned manner.

Although I was elated at our discovery, I was also saddened by this incident. Trevor didn't even know that he was being shot at. This whole incident could have been avoided if he had left earlier from Georgia and wasn't tired. This guy didn't even have a chance.

I call Mr. and Mrs. Chase to tell them our discovery however when they asked to see the footage I recommend to them that they not view it, so they took my advice and chose not to view it. To actually see your child being murdered is such a devastating feeling that one cannot ever forget. It is engrained in the mind and the soul. I believe that this would have caused more harm and damage to the Chase's than it would have helped them, so even though I could not stop them from viewing the footage, I am glad that they had listened to me and chose not to.

Chapter 30

The State hired a private legal team for Officer Rand which is usually very unheard of since the State does have its own set of lawyers for such matters. It was very obvious that the three attorneys that the State hired were highly paid decorative counsel. They are what we in the legal field would call Super Lawyers. It was also very obvious that the State wanted to do whatever it took for them to win this case. It's just unfortunate that it is the taxpayer's money that is flipping the bill.

As we picked the jurors to hear this case, my mind recollects back to the Whinebeck case when we did the jury selection back then. Wow, so much has changed, so much was different in my life back then. If that jury back then was different, I may not have won, and Rodney would have still been in jail the night Ciana was hit. Realizing that I get very emotional every time I think about that moment, I divert my thinking so that I could concentrate on the outcome I wish for this case to go. I have to always remember what Ciana had told me when she said that she was okay and wanted me to continue with my purpose, so I must do just that.

I soon find out that picking a jury for a civil case is so much different than picking one for a criminal case. Although we only needed six jurors as opposed to the twelve needed in a criminal case, I found it more difficult to choose those right individuals. The respondent's lawyers are way more seasoned at this than I am. When it comes to millions of dollars that could be won or lost, jury selection is an art to be mastered and they are definitely the masters here.

I was trying to get at least two Black jurors however we ended up with four white men, one white woman, and one Latino woman on the jury. The odds definitely don't seem to be in our favor. How would any of these jurors even know what it would be like to be stopped by a police officer just because you are black? They never experienced the difficulties that Black people have with law enforcement officials for no apparent reason or what's it like to be presumed guilty of something even though you might not have done anything wrong. Most of them think that police officers are usually right ninety-nine percent of the time in their actions and there must be some reason why they do what they do. I, somehow, am going to have to find, and strive to show them that one percent of misconduct.

When we start the trial, Federal Judge McAllister presides over the case. I've never met this judge before, so I don't have any experience or much knowledge as to how he does his trials. All I do know from the research that I had done on him is that he is ultra conservative. He once ruled against an African American woman who filed a civil rights suit against a white supremist man who she had been employed with. She had claimed that because the man was racist, he kept her from advancing as quickly as her white counterparts. Although the man admitted that he was "pro-white" he stated that he hired her because he believed in her abilities and was disappointed that she did not reach the potential that he believed that she could reach.

Judge McAllister questions everyone to see if we are all ready to begin the trial, and then tells me to proceed with my opening statement for the jury.

The funny thing about that is that as a criminal defense attorney I had always gone second, never first.

In a criminal trial the prosecutor opens with the opening statement first and then the defense goes second, so it was easy to tailor my statement based on what the prosecutor would say. Here in a civil case, it's the plaintiff who goes first. Now that I am with the plaintiff I am the one to set the tone.

"May it please the Court, Your Honor?"

"You may proceed, please." Judge McAllister answered.

"Thank you, Your Honor." I say as I proceed with my opening statement. "Good morning, Your Honor, Counsel, and ladies and gentlemen of the jury. I first would like to thank you for your patience and also thank you for your service on this jury. I am Richard Clayton, the attorney for the plaintiffs, Mr. Robert Chase and Mrs. Belinda Chase, who filed a civil action on behalf of their deceased son, Trevor Chase, against police officer Ronald Rand and the Maryland State Police for the excessive use of force performed by Officer Rand which caused the death of Trevor. – When we have children, we teach them to respect their parents, the elderly, and the police. We tell our children that police officers are here to help us, and protect us, and we can call on them whenever we need help because they are trained to protect us from those who are out to do wrong. When children see police officers, they hold them in very high adulation and respect, and usually the police officers inspire these children to do good in school and uphold the law. Trevor Chase did exactly that. He had never been in trouble with the law not even a speeding ticket! And, he had earned two scholarships for school, one in athletics and the other in academics. He always respected police officers and the law and stayed away from wrongdoing. The first and only one in his family to go to college, he was on a mission to succeed as a civil engineer and make his family proud. When Officer Rand pulled Trevor over that early morning, Trevor complied with the officer's wishes even though he was unsure as to why he was being pulled over. When Officer Rand felt as though Trevor wasn't listening to his demands anymore, he pulls out his weapon and shoots at Trevor, not one time, not two times, not even three times, but sixteen times! Sixteen times for one man who is not even shooting back. Thirteen of those bullets hit Trevor. Ten hit his torso and extremities, three hit him directly in the head. That's not only uncalled for, it is unacceptable. Your verdict will speak to society and tell police what is acceptable and what isn't. Thank you."

I return to the Plaintiff table and watch as one of the three attorneys for the Defense approach the jury booth. The jury watches the female attorney intensely as she approaches them. Her blond hair is perfectly put together, and she wears a black pinned-striped suit that is sexy yet very professional, she looks as though she stepped right out of a glamour magazine. With a jury that consists of four white men I can see why they chose her to open.

"Good morning, Your Honor, Counsel, and ladies and gentlemen of the jury. I am Jennifer Stevens, and I'm here to prove to you that Officer Rand was justified in his actions and why, although tragic, the

State is not responsible for the death of Mr. Trevor Chase. What is this case about? This case is about an officer who felt the need to defend himself by any means necessary. This is an officer who has been on the force for nearly ten years protecting citizens and enforcing the law against crime. This officer did everything right according to police protocol. When you view the body cam video, you will see that he spoke calmly to Mr. Chase. You will see that it was Mr. Chase who was annoyed and agitated because he was stopped by a police officer. Yes, as Plaintiff's counsel mentioned, we teach our children to respect law enforcement officers. If my son were ever pulled over, he is taught to be friendly to the officer. Mr. Chase was not friendly to the officer and therefore the officer felt threatened from the start. There was no excessive force here. The officer did exactly what was needed in order to subdue the situation. Thank you."

"Plaintiff, present your first evidence." Stated Judge McAllister.

"Yes, your Honor." I say. "We would like to first present to you the officer's body cam video and break it down for the jury."

I set the monitor up so that the jury and the judge are able to perfectly view the video from where they are sitting. I hold the remote in my hand so that I could pause the video whenever I needed to discuss something.

PLAY

[Trevor: Hey officer, what's up?

Officer: Good morning, I am fitted with a body cam, so all conversation and actions are being recorded. I need your driver's license and your car registration.

Trevor: Um, sir, can you tell me why I was pulled over for?

Officer: I'll tell you after you give me your driver's license and your car registration.]

PAUSE

It starts right here. The contention that the officer has for Trevor. Trevor is calm and friendly. He greets the officer appropriately and kindly asks the officer why he was pulled over for.

PLAY

[Trevor: I need a minute to get them, officer. – -- Here you go. So, can you tell me now why I was pulled over?

Officer: Have you been drinking?

Trevor: No.

Officer: Have you taken any type of drugs whether illegal or prescription?

Trevor: No!

Officer: I clocked you at 80 miles per hour and also noticed that you were weaving the lanes. Why are your eyes bloodshot and your speech slurred?]

PAUSE

"Again, Trevor is calm and complying with the officer. The officer insinuates that Trevor must be intoxicated or drug induced because his eyes are bloodshot, and his speech is slurred." I express to the jury.

PLAY

[Trevor: I had been driving for about ten hours from Atlanta, so I'm extremely tired.

Officer: Do you have any drugs or weapons in the vehicle?

Trevor: What? No!

Officer: You are very fidgety which makes me think that you are either hiding something in the car or you are under the influence of a narcotic or alcohol.]
PAUSE

"Here Trevor explains to the officer that he has been on the road for ten hours. He explains that he is just tired. The officer doesn't adhere to what he is saying. He accuses Trevor of hiding something. Which, of course, nothing was ever found." I explain.
PLAY

[Trevor: What the hell! I'm not hiding shit, I'm just super sleepy.

Officer: Then you won't mind if I do a quick little search of the vehicle do you?

Trevor: Yes, I do mind. No, you can't search my car.

Officer: Look, all I have to do is to call for an officer to bring a dog here to walk around your vehicle and if the K-9 alerts me to let me know that something is in the vehicle I will let the judge and the prosecutor know of your lack of cooperation. At least if you tell me now I can be more lenient on you.]
PAUSE

"Here is where Trevor starts to get agitated. He complied with the officer all the way until here when the officer kept insinuating that Trevor was committing some type of crime. Then the officer goes to the point of trying to intimidate Trevor by telling him that he has the power to influence a judge and a prosecutor."
PLAY

[Trevor: Go right ahead then. Call a dog unit here. I'm not going to allow you to search my car.

Officer: (squeezing the button of his radio attached to his collar) Requesting backup. Possible 10-50 or 10-51, need a K-9 unit.]
PAUSE

"Because Trevor is not intimidated by the officer, the officer calls for backup. He states that there is a possible 10-50 which means suspect is under the influence of narcotics, and a 10-51 which means subject is intoxicated, then asks for a K-9 unit. Mind you, all this even after Trevor stated that he was just super tired from driving over ten hours from Georgia."
PLAY

[Officer: Wait here.

Trevor: I'm not going anywhere.

Officer goes into his car and inputs information into the computer. Approximately 8 minutes later, Trevor's car is seen going backwards. Officer then jumps out of his vehicle with weapon drawn.

Officer: STOP YOUR VEHICLE! STOP YOUR VEHICLE! STOP NOW! STOP!

POW! POW! POW! POW! POW! POW! POW! POW! POW! POW! POW! POW! POW! POW! POW! POW!

Officer: (speaking into his radio) 10-57, shots fired! Shots fired! Possible 10-53.]
STOP

"Sixteen shots fired! Did you count them? Bang, Bang, Bang, Bang, Bang, Bang, Bang, Bang, Bang, Bang, Bang, Bang, Bang, Bang, Bang! – Sixteen! – Thank you." I say using my fingers as a gun acting as if I'm firing. I then return back to my table.

The second attorney for the defense stands up to cross-examine the video. He is a very tall astute white male with a voice spoken with cold formality with a timbre of upper-class arrogance and measured cadences.

"As we watched the video, Officer Rand told Mr. Chase the full reason why he was pulled over. When Mr. Chase didn't like the answer, he got agitated. It is right here." The attorney says as he plays back a certain section of the video.

[Officer: I clocked you at 80 miles per hour and also notice that you were weaving the lanes. Why are your eyes bloodshot and your speech slurred?]

"He told Mr. Chase his reason and had politely asked him if he was under the influence of anything. As a trained officer of the law, he is able to know whether someone is just tired or if they are under some form of influence. He was acting according to his training. Then he tells Mr. Chase that he does not feel safe and would like to inspect his vehicle. Mr. Chase refuses. Now if one doesn't have anything to hide, why not just let the officer check? When the officer is refused to do so and returns to his car to run Mr. Chase's information, Mr. Chase's car comes barreling down towards the officer. Now, if I was a police officer and the person I stopped won't allow me to check their vehicle and then all of a sudden, their car is racing towards mine, I would do whatever I could to defend myself. The officer wasn't sure what was going on. This man could have been an escaped convict not wanting to get caught. The officer needed to subdue the suspect as quickly as possible. – Thank you."

"Plaintiff, please present your next witness or next piece of evidence." Judge McAllister tells me.

"The second piece of evidence in which the Plaintiff would like to present is the dash-cam from the squad car." I tell the jury. "Although the camera automatically starts to record as soon as the flashing patrol lights are turned on, I will not play the whole video but would rather just play the part when the shooting takes place."

The video starts and is fast forwarded to when Trevor's car starts to roll backwards.

"Look!" I tell the jury. "His brake lights are on at first and then they are off. This means that his foot was removed from the brake pedal. Also, notice that there are no white lights. This means that he did not put the car in reverse. I also want you to look very closely at his head. Here, I'll try to blow up the image so that you can see it better. First his head tilts backwards, and then cocks to the right. He didn't hear the police officer telling him to stop because he fell asleep. He was sleeping folks! Instead of the officer investigating the situation he fires his weapon, sixteen times! – Thank you."

"Would the defense like to cross-examine Plaintiff's exhibit number two?" asked Judge McAllister.

"Yes, Your Honor, Defense would." Stated the same tall male attorney as previously.

"I want you all to imagine this. You are a police officer working the graveyard shift and you know and realize that most violent crime happens during that time. More than likely you are going to be more vigilant and cognizant about your surroundings and what you do. This is a very dangerous job. Each day is a gamble with your life. So, you pull someone over and they do not fully comply with what you ask them to do. You then ask if you could check their vehicle and they refuse. Now you see this car barreling down towards you. Look at this video. Imagine if you were in that squad car and all you see is a car coming to you swiftly. What do you do to save your life? You will react. If you look at the video, the squad car's spotlight is so bright that one wouldn't be able to tell if he let go of the break or not, and at the speed that Mr. Chase's car was going, it is very hard to see if the reverse lights were on or not. – Thank you."

"Does the Plaintiff have any more witnesses or pieces of evidence?" Judge McAllister asks me.

"No Your Honor, we do not." I tell him.

"Does the defense have any witnesses or pieces of evidence that they would like to present?" asked Judge McAllister to the defense.

"Your Honor, we are going to call Officer Rand to the stand to testify." Jennifer stated.

The bailiff goes to the hall and calls in Officer Rand into the courtroom. In walks a very tall astute man wearing his full-dress police uniform with his wide brim "Smokey" hat under his left arm. The sounds of the taps on his shoes clicking on the hardwood floor made everyone in the courtroom watch him as he walks up to the witness stand with his right hand already posed to say the oath.

"Officer Rand, could you please tell us in your own words what happened on the night in question when you pulled over Trevor Chase?" asked Jennifer.

Officer Rand pauses and then clears his throat before speaking.

"It was about 1:30 in the morning when I was sitting in the median strip along interstate 95 close to exit 36 facing northbound, when I observed a vehicle speeding at 80 miles per hour. I then pulled my vehicle out and drove a little distance behind the vehicle before turning on my emergency flashing lights. As I was following the vehicle, I notice that the driver seemed to be weaving the lanes, so after about a mile I then turned on my flashing lights. When the driver noticed my flashing lights, he pulled over his vehicle to the right shoulder of the interstate. When I approached the vehicle to ask the driver questions as well as to obtain his license and registration, I notice that the driver's speech was very slurred, and his eyes were bloodshot and was squinting as if he was high. I had then asked the driver if he was under the influence of anything or had he been using any type of marijuana since I smelled an odor coming from the vehicle when he rolled down the window. The occupant, Mr. Chase, seemed to become very hostile with me because I was asking him these very relevant questions. When he didn't allow me to search him or his vehicle I had gotten very suspicious and started to fear for my own safety. After questioning him, I returned to my vehicle to run his information. As I'm sitting there waiting for the information to come back, I notice that his vehicle is coming at me full force, so I jump out of my vehicle and yell for him to stop his vehicle. When he was refusing to stop, I fired my weapon into his vehicle."

"Officer Rand, did you feel threatened at any time?"

"Yes, ma'am. I felt very threatened."

"At what point did you start to feel threatened?" asked Jennifer.

"Well, when I pulled him over, I wasn't sure exactly what to expect. He seemed very fidgety and as if he were under the influence of something, and usually when someone is under the influence of anything there is a serious threat that can be imposed."

"Did you notice anything unusual when you pulled him over?" Jennifer asked.

"Well, his eyes were bloodshot, and his speech was a bit slurred. These are indicators that someone may be under the influence of either drugs or alcohol. Also, I thought that I could smell a slight scent of marijuana. This is why I needed to search the vehicle."

"What were you thinking when he refused to allow you to search his vehicle?"

"I immediately felt that he was hiding something."

"When you went back to your vehicle what were you doing?"

"I entered his information into several different databases so that I would be able to know if there were any outstanding warrants in other states. It is a process doing so, so it takes a little time for everything to come back."

"Was this what was happening when Mr. Chase rammed his vehicle into yours?"

"Yes, I was trying to obtain information on him at that time. When I saw his vehicle come swiftly towards mine, I had to jump out and yell for him to stop."

"What were you thinking at the time when you saw his vehicle coming towards you?"

"Well, I thought that there might have been some information that he didn't want me to find out about, so honestly I thought that he was trying to kill me because he thought that I would have found out something about him."

"So at that time, did you feel that you were going to be killed?"

"Yes, I did. That is why I fired my weapon at him in order to try to stop him."

"Thank you, no further questions."

"Redirect?" Judge McAllister asked me.

"Yes, Your Honor." I state.

"Officer Rand, you stated in your testimony that you felt threatened by Mr. Chase when you pulled him over. What was the exact moment when you felt threatened?"

"Well, as I mentioned before, I felt threatened when I approached him because he seemed a bit agitated."

"I'm not fully understanding this. Why would you feel threatened when you have not seen any weapon or anything that could physically harm you?"

"Well, because when people are under the influence of drugs or alcohol, they can be very erratic in their actions and behavior."

"Erratic in their actions and behavior? Trevor Chase was 5 foot 7 inches tall weighing in about 140 pounds, you are clearly over 6 feet and probably weigh at least 220 pounds. Please explain what kind of erratic actions that he could have had without a weapon and you couldn't stop him without one?"

"Look, I don't know. My instincts were just telling me that he could do something crazy."

"So, when his car rolled backwards, because you were expecting him to do something erratic, you automatically assumed that he was ramming your car, is that correct to say?" I asked.

"Well yes, for the most part."

"Tell me this, why did you have to shoot sixteen times?"

"I had warned him to stop. He was not listening. He was threatening an officer of the law, so I fired."

"Yes, you did. Sixteen times. No further questions."

"Does the defense have any more witnesses or evidence to present?" asked Judge McAllister.

"Yes, we do, your Honor."

"Proceed." stated Judge McAllister.

"We would like to present the toxicology report from the autopsy of Mr. Chase that we received from the Office of the Chief Medical Examiner. As you can see here, Mr. Chase was shown positive for marijuana and amphetamine. This proves the officer's actions were justified. Mr. Chase was under the influence of drugs and because of that, he recklessly tried to ram a police officer's car. He might not have known what he was doing, but it wasn't because of being sleepy, it was because he was drug induced. Don't let the Plaintiff fool you into thinking that Mr. Chase was this holier than thou great law-abiding kid, he wasn't. Marijuana and amphetamines?? Doesn't look like he was all that law-abiding. Does it? Thank you."

"Would the Plaintiff like to cross?" asked Judge McAllister.

"Yes, your Honor." I say, clearly a bit miffed and annoyed as to how this woman spoke as if she personally knew Trevor. I didn't even know him personally and I felt offended by what she had said. I can just imagine what Trevor's parents must be thinking after that statement.

"When I first saw the toxicology report, I'll be honest with you. I was a bit disappointed. I thought to myself, drugs. Anything but drugs. Then I realized what we were dealing with and what this case is about. This is a 21-year-old kid in college. How many of you remember those good ole college days? Sex, drugs, and rock and roll! This does not negate the fact as to whether Officer Rand used excessive force or not. Hypothetically, even if Trevor was drug induced at the time of the incident, should excessive force really have been used?

The toxicology report did not state a percentage or how much was in his system, it just stated that there was a positive trace of the drug. Let me remind you that marijuana can stay in the system for up to thirty days. This does not state that he was high at the time of the incident. Thank you."

"If neither the Plaintiff nor the Defense have any other witnesses or evidence to present then please proceed with your closing arguments." stated Judge McAllister.

I approach the jury box in order to present my closing argument. I'm still feeling a bit frazzled over how the defense portrayed Trevor. She did this intentional not only for the jury but to try to trip me up. When I was doing criminal defense, it was so much easier. I was confident in myself and knew how to defeat my opponents, here I feel out of my league and I believe the defense knows it. God told me that I must do my purpose. If I do what God tells me I know that I will be successful. I need to get my confidence back. I think about Ciana. I think about Trevor. I think about my purpose. Now I must deliver.

"Ladies and gentlemen of the jury, despite the Defense's exculpatory tone, they know in their hearts that shooting a man sixteen times is excessive. The definition of excessive force is that a law enforcement officer has the right to use such force as is reasonably necessary under the circumstances to make a lawful arrest. Let me repeat that. Reasonably – necessary – under – the – circumstances – to – make – a – lawful – arrest. Shooting someone sixteen times is not reasonably necessary. This was not done in the line of duty. Even if the officer felt as though his life was threatened, why not just shoot twice then jump out of the way. What would have been the difference in the outcome that he thought would happen if he only shot twice? Did he think that Trevor would keep reversing his car until he was able to hit the officer? Trevor was not only a law-abiding citizen, Trevor was a good student. A junior in college, an honor student, and an athlete. He received a full scholarship because of his academics and received a full scholarship for his game on the basketball court. He was so determined to reach home that day to see his parents and his younger brother and sister. He was very excited to reach because he was starting a new internship at the Department of Transportation in Washington DC two days later. This was a kid who stayed out of trouble and wanted to accomplish something major in his life. Sixteen bullets cut his life short. This should not have happened. Your verdict will say to the State; NO! This is unacceptable. Your verdict must punish the State for allowing this action, so it will never ever happen again. – The Plaintiff rests its case."

As I sit back down to wait for the Defense's closing argument, I try to read the juror's faces. I don't see one face that seems to be swayed by what I had said. I notice that as soon as Jennifer stands up to approach, she had captured their attention immediately. Now I'm thinking that maybe I made a mistake in not having taken the settlement offer. I hope, win or lose, that Mr. and Mrs. Chase know how much of a hard effort that I put in. I really hope that they know that I did my ultimate best.

"Good afternoon, ladies and gentlemen, we spent the day here trying to figure out as to whether Officer Rand operated appropriately or not, and whether he was within his rights as a law enforcement officer to subdue a subject that he felt threatened by. Let's look at the facts here. Officer Rand pulled over a driver for driving erratically. When he confronted the driver, the driver became hostile and agitated. Then the officer became even more suspicious when the driver refused to allow him to search the vehicle as if Mr. Chase had something to hide. Now, when Officer Rand gets to his car, the Plaintiff wants us to believe that Mr. Chase just so happens to fall asleep and his car just happens to roll back into the squad car? Hogwash! Usually if one gets stopped by an officer they become fully alert. Even if Mr. Chase just happened to fall asleep, Officer

Rand cannot be liable whatsoever because there is no way that he could tell if the vehicle is being reversed or if it is being rolled back because of the intensity and brightness of the spotlight on the squad car. The officer nor the state is liable. Officer Rand was just doing his job. He was doing his job as an official police officer, serving and protecting society. Officer Rand felt as though his life was threatened and did what it took to subdue the situation. If you all find fault in his duties as a policeman, this will send the message to all police officers that they will not be able to do their job in protecting you from nefarious criminals. The Defense rests."

Judge McAllister gives the jury instructions and then dismisses them for deliberations. I decide to leave the building and grab a bite to eat since I had not eaten anything all day. Jeremiah comes with me and helps me carry my files. He sees the stress and worn on my face and decides to not say too much unless I ask him something. I see Mr. and Mrs. Chase in the hallway and try to avoid eye contact with them. Jeremiah and I go to a little café to eat and to wait until the court calls to let us know when the jury would be done with its deliberation and has reached a verdict. Jeremiah and I sit in a booth and wait not saying a word. After two and a half hours, my cell phone rings. It's the Court letting us know that the verdict is in. Jeremiah and I gather our things calmly and head back to the courthouse. The moment of truth is here.

Chapter 31

When Jeremiah and I reach back to the courthouse, there was a massive crowd of protesters outside the building with signs yelling for justice.

A small, young African American woman is yelling on a bullhorn, "No Justice, No Peace!" in cadence with a voice that has a trace of huskiness and with a hint of more power than her small body would suggest.

Councilman Raymond Watts is standing on the entrance pathway speaking to a group of reporters but when they see me and Jeremiah coming back to go inside the building, they rush over to us and bombard me with questions in which I refuse to answer and keep walking.

As I walk into the courtroom, the Judge is sitting at the bench working on some papers with his law clerk. Mr. and Mrs. Chase are already sitting down in their seats so I walk over to them and briefly put my hand on Mr. Chase's shoulder and then take my seat at the Plaintiff's table.

"All rise for the jury," yelled the court clerk as she opened the door to let the jurors back into the courtroom from their deliberations. As the six jurors walk back into the courtroom and take their seats in the jury box, I try once again to try to read their facial expression to see if I could get a feeling for what direction that the verdict is leaning. Of course, I am still unable to read them.

The jurors walk in stoned face without making any eye contact with neither me nor the Defense. Usually when someone in the jury makes eye contact with someone on either side, that particular side usually wins. Here, they made no eye contact with either one of us. I look back in the pews and see Mr. and Mrs. Chase holding hands with their heads down as if they are praying. I then look at Jeremiah who looks at me first with concern, and then with admiration, as if to say; 'Keep your head up. You did your best.'

The three Super Lawyers for the Defense just sit back in their chairs confidently feeling the fruit of their bearings, however, Officer Rand actually looks a bit guilty. I really wonder what is going on in his head. Does he have any remorse for killing someone who really didn't deserve it? I really wonder that. It's like Raymond Whinebeck. Did Raymond have any feelings of guilt knowing that the one who helped him he killed? He killed a part of my soul when he killed Ciana, and I just really wonder if he has any remorse.

The foreman hands a slip of paper over to the bailiff to hand to the judge. Judge McAllister looks at the folded paper and reads the verdict to himself and then hands it to the court clerk. The clerk stands and speaks loud for everyone in the courtroom to hear her.

"In the case of Chase v. State of Maryland, Rand et el., the jury finds in favor of the Plaintiff, four to two."

Oh my God!! I won the case! Thank you, God!!

The clerk continues; "The jury awards the Plaintiff 4.5 million dollars in compensatory damages and 2.5 million dollars in punitive damages."

Holy shit! Seven million dollars!! My knees weaken but I hold my composure and act confidently in the decision made by the jury. I look over at Mr. and Mrs. Chase and see that they are holding their hands up thanking God, and then I look over at Jeremiah and his facial expression says; See, I told you!

The courtroom erupts in cheers and everyone is shaking my hand congratulating me on my win. When I leave out of the courtroom reporters and camera are in the hall. I see Counselman Watts speaking to some of them, and then as the reporters see me, again they all rush towards me.

"This is a win for all the men and women who were wrongfully and innocently killed by police officers where no justice was served. I thank everyone for their support." I say to the reporters and cameras.

I then rush out to my car and sit for a moment before starting the car. I then start the car and drive to Ciana's resting place. When I finally reach her gravesite, I sit next to it remembering her presence in my "dream" and what so told me; 'Complete my purpose.'

"You always believe me, Ciana. You will always be in my heart. I will love you always."

ABOUT THE AUTHOR

Leopole McLaughlin is a serial entrepreneur with several business ventures and who has authored several published non-fiction books. These books include;

Zero to a Million in 12, the 12 Step Guide to Making a Million Dollars in a Year;
Winning the Baby Mamma Drama Dilemma;
Playing the Game;
When Dealing with Snakes become a Mongoose; and
The Super Achiever.

Two Strands of Light is Leopole McLaughlin's debut fiction publication.

A Beacon of Light coming out December 2020.

Made in the USA
Middletown, DE
19 September 2021

48635821R00132